BREATH OF CORRUPTION

Caro Fraser was educated in Glasgow and the Isle of Man. She worked as an advertising copywriter for a number of years before reading law at King's College, London University, and was called to the Bar of Middle Temple in 1979. She is the author of twelve other novels, six of which are part of the highly successful, critically acclaimed Caper Court series. She lives in London with her husband and four children.

Breath of Corruption

CARO FRASER

Matador
9 De Montfort Mews
Leicester LE1 7FW, UK
Tel: (+44) 116 255 9311 / 9312
Email: books@troubador.co.uk
Web: www.troubador.co.uk/matador

ISBN 978-1906221-232

Typeset in 11pt Garamond by Troubador Publishing Ltd, Leicester, UK
Printed in the UK by The Cromwell Press Ltd, Trowbridge, Wilts, UK

Matador is an imprint of Troubador Publishing Ltd

With affectionate thanks to Ian Simpson and
Tim Young for all their invaluable help.

1

A silky blue haze of summer smog lay over London. Along New Bond Street slow herds of taxis and delivery vans grunted and roared from one set of lights to another, sending diesel fumes and CO_2 emissions and invisible clouds of human exasperation drifting heavenwards to add to the noxious ether. Dispassionately the drivers watched the muscled arrogance of the cycle couriers as they wove and sped through the stationary traffic, and eyed the expensively-clad women clicking along the pavements in tiny heels and summer dresses, faces disdainful and preoccupied behind designer sunglasses. All human traffic seemed to move faster than the lines of vehicles.

The time was ten to one, and office workers were beginning to spill on to the street and into Pret a Manger and Costa Coffee. Down in the cool, chic basement restaurant of Nicole Farhi, at a peaceful remove from the street clamour of crashing gears and hissing hydraulic brakes up above, tranquillity reigned. Here the only sounds were those of tinkling cutlery and murmuring female voices. Stylish young waitresses moved about, sliding plates of salads on to tables and uncapping chilled bottles of mineral water, while the lunching ladies paused their conversation to watch as the water burbled into their glasses, its discreet fizz heralding the delicious thrill of shared gossip and exchanged confidences.

At one table, and one table alone, was wine being consumed. A bottle of Gavi, light and luscious, and with its own hint of fizz, was already two-thirds empty, and the salads had yet to arrive. Anthea Grieves-Brown lifted the bottle from the wine chiller and glugged the remains into her own glass and that of her friend, Lola Canning. She tucked strands of blonde hair, straightened and smoothed to the sheen of satin, behind one ear as she leaned forward to murmur by way of addition to her previous observation, 'Four times in one night.' She articulated the sentiment with slow wonder, and a catlike, satisfied smile widened her beautiful features as she waited for her friend's reaction.

Lola made an unimpressed face. Man-less herself at the moment, feigning boredom was the only way she knew to counter the envy and irritation she felt as Anthea recounted the charms of her latest man and his amazing prowess in bed. 'But isn't that rather showing off? Reminds me of the dreadful Cherie telling us that Tony Blair was a five-times-a-night man. Ghastly.' She took a swig of her wine. 'Suggests he has something to prove.'

Anthea deflected this attempted put-down. 'Obviously, darling, if it's the same man you've been with for ages and ages, the last thing you want is to have him jump all over you at three o'clock in the morning. But you could never put Leo Davies in that category. Not in a million years.'

Lola swallowed a sigh and gave a tight, bright smile. The unwritten code of female friendship stated that one was obliged to indulge with forbearance, if not enthusiasm, the raptures of friends newly in love, and so remarks of encouragement and gestures expressive of interest were the order of the day. Little murmurs of envy were generally acceptable, too, but since Lola didn't feel moved to articulate a sentiment which she was in danger of feeling all too sincerely, she merely said, 'Tell me more about this wonderful man. What does he do, apart from make the earth move four times a night?'

'He's a QC – you know, one of those important barrister people.'

'I do know what a QC is – my father used to be one.'

'So he was... Anyway, Leo told me the kind of work he does, but I wasn't really paying much attention. We were in bed at the time.' Another greedy smile lit up Anthea's face. 'God, I can't tell you, Lola – it's *so* absolutely the best sex I've ever had.'

'That's saying something, certainly, given the numbers.'

'I mean, *just* amazing... Anyway, whatever he does is to do with ships and stuff, and other people's money. Sounds very dull, but it must earn him a complete fortune, because he drives an Aston Martin and has a house near Cheyne Walk. There's regularly stuff in the papers about QCs who earn squillions, so I assume he's one of them.'

At that moment lunch arrived. Anthea inspected her salad and then glanced at the little jug of dressing on the side. 'God, I absolutely don't want that. Take it away,' she said to the waitress.

Lola added, 'And bring us another bottle of this.' The waitress took the empty bottle and disappeared. A bottle was far more than anyone should drink at lunchtime, Lola knew, but sod it – Anthea, who was meant to be living on a model's diet of egg whites and mineral water, didn't care, so neither did she. There wasn't anything else to do with the day, anyway. Maybe they'd wobble along to the Curzon afterwards and slip into a late afternoon film. Then home for a nap, up at nine to shower and beautify, and out on the town for such pleasures as the rest of the night might yield. A wealthy family and a trust fund did give one a charmed life, but even Lola found it boring occasionally – though alcohol and the odd recreational drug helped take the edge off the tedium. In the long years since leaving her Swiss finishing school, Lola had often thought she should get herself some not-too-demanding job – something involving flexible hours and long lunches, and a stylish office with a PA – but that meant working, and genuine work didn't really appeal. And to be honest, at thirty-one, she was a bit scared that whatever skills she'd once possessed might be a bit rusty by now. Some of her friends ran fashions shops and glam little businesses, but that took effort, too. And ideas. If she'd had Anthea's long legs and amazingly slim figure, not to mention her looks, she'd have been able to do a little casual modelling, too. Anthea needed the money, of course, but the job had a certain cachet, and gave her something else to talk about.

3

'What does he look like?'

Anthea reflected, fork paused above her salad. 'He's sort of moderately tall, I suppose – about five eleven? And rather unusual looking. I mean, he has the most divine face – lovely square jaw and beautiful cheekbones, and the most *utterly*, piercingly sexy blue eyes – but his hair is completely grey. Well, more silver actually. Rather strange, given his age, but really quite cool.'

'How old is he?'

Anthea shrugged. 'Mid-forties.'

'Wife?'

'Ex.'

'Kids?'

'One, little boy of four, lives with mummy.'

'Psychological flaws?'

'None I can detect. Unless you count the fact that he's Welsh.'

'He shags sheep.'

Anthea tilted her lovely head to one side, and smiled. 'It's just the faintest accent. Rather sexy, actually. Gives his voice a hint of menace. Like Anthony Hopkins.'

'You're mad. Or in love.'

Anthea lifted her glass and arched her brow. 'You know me, Lolly. I'm not into love. The original material girl.'

'So this Leo isn't a long-term proposition?'

'I didn't say that. One can make a mid to long-term investment without being in love.' She shrugged. 'In my experience, love just screws things up. People getting all needy and insecure.'

'So where did you meet him?'

'You remember Muriel, who used to live with Jeremy?'

'The sculptress?'

'Right. Well, she had an exhibition at the White Cube and invited loads of us to the opening, and I met him there. Lust at first sight. He was seriously into the art – I was seriously into the champagne. We went back to his afterwards, and that was it.'

'Ant, you're the most terrible old tart, you know – jumping

4

into bed with men as soon as you clap eyes on them.'

'Believe me, if you'd been there, you would have too. Anyway, I'm not. I've been out with him four times since, and each time *he*'s called *me*.'

'Been out with, or been to bed with?'

'Out first, bed after. Twice to the theatre – '

'You? At the theatre?'

'I know. It was just incredibly dull. He's a bit of an intellectual. I think he thinks I am too.'

'He can't possibly!'

'Love you too, Lolly.' Anthea poured more wine. 'It's because we met at an exhibition, and despite what you may think, I can say all the right things without necessarily knowing a great deal.'

'One of your many talents.'

'Indeed. Anyway, it's worth sitting through Proust or whatever for a meal at Petrus and the sex afterwards.'

'He sounds too good to be true. Enjoy it while it lasts.'

'Don't worry, darling. I know how to keep his attention. In bed and out of it. My latest tactic is playing hard-to-get.'

'Isn't it a bit late for that?'

Anthea smiled. 'Trust me – everything I do is timed to perfection. By the time the weekend's over he'll be aching to see me.'

2

A mile or so away from the restaurant where Anthea and Lola were lunching, wedged between the clamour of Fleet Street and the grey meander of the Thames, another oasis of tranquillity basked in the heat of late August – the Temple. This venerable sprawl of ancient buildings, sombre alleyways, shadowed courtyards, echoing staircases and sunlit gardens, has for centuries been home to those who toil in the service of the law. Theirs is a task of dedication, for the machinery of English justice is complex and ponderous, and constant vigilance is required to ensure that it does not buckle or break beneath the weight of its own responsibility. Its little cogs and flywheels are oiled daily, and its component parts kept running smoothly by the clerks who make and take phone calls, scurry between courts and chambers, and negotiate business on behalf of the barristers; the barristers in turn see to it that the pistons pump healthily and the valves open and close with polished regularity by perusing briefs, consulting authorities, delivering learned opinions and appearing in court; Her Majesty's judges of The Supreme Court of England and Wales preside with admirable sedulity over the machine's churning output of judgments, awards and practice directions, and voluminous by-products of hot air and ashy waste are generated by City solicitors over-feeding the furnace with mounds of files, letters and papers.

The very names appended to the buildings, courtyards and alleyways – Serjeant's Inn, King's Bench Walk, Crown Office Row, Dr Johnson's Buildings – are evocative of its ancient history, and through its dappled courtyards, stone-flagged lanes and dreaming gardens the shadows of long-dead inhabitants seem still to flit – those eminent jurists, Coke, Halsbury and

Littleton, and the great men of letters, Thackeray, Lamb and Goldsmith. Yet the barristers' chambers situated in the Temple are not mired in ancient practices; they operate in the present day with the stream-lined, globalised efficiency of any multi-national organisation, and though clad for their work within the courts in horsehair wigs and flowing gowns, the barristers themselves are generally sophisticated, worldly metropolitan beings.

One such being was Leo Davies, a forty-six year-old commercial barrister who, besides being possessed of all the personal attractions adverted to by Anthea Grieves-Brown over lunch, held a high reputation amongst his fellow lawyers for his forensic skills and powers of rhetoric, not to mention his charm, wit and charismatic personality. Leo had only a year ago been made head of chambers at number 5 Caper Court, and now presided over some thirty tenants, ranging from eminent QCs at the top end, ambitious senior juniors in the middle, and junior barristers and raw recruits, known as pupils, at the bottom.

Caper Court itself, originally laid out by Sir Christopher Wren in the years following the Great Fire of London, was a quaint courtyard with archways leading to Middle Temple Lane at one end and Pump Court at the other, and its buildings housed five different sets of chambers. On the top floor of number 9 Caper Court, which stood on the other side of the courtyard facing number 5, a beautiful old sundial was set in the brickwork, inscribed with the melancholy sentiment, 'Shadows we are and like shadows depart,' and on this summer day Leo was standing at his window and gazing across at the inscription, familiar to him for over twenty five years, with particular pensiveness.

He had fallen into one of those occasional moods in which the routine of his work took on an uncharacteristic dreariness, and the point of existence seemed to escape him. Behind him on his desk, next to his computer screen, lay papers relating to a case involving a contract for the carriage c.i.f. of soya bean pellets to Montoir. Normally the minutiae of the contractual details and exacting issues as to jurisdiction would have exerted their familiar fascination, but today, as he watched the sunshine creep across the gilded Roman numerals of the sundial, such considerations seemed petty and irrelevant. It occurred to him that perhaps he felt this way because his inner man was in need of nourishment. Maybe he should go and get a sandwich or a cup of coffee. Or, better still, rustle up Michael Gibbon to share a glass of wine and the latest gossip at El Vino's. Not that many people drank at lunchtime any more. The departure of the journalists to Canary Wharf and the arrival of the New Labour Puritan ethic had seen to that.

His ruminations were interrupted by a light knock on the door and the arrival of one of the clerks. Felicity, a bright, bosomy, bustling young woman with a tendency to disorganisation which she managed to keep in check only by ferocious concentration and reminders muttered below her breath, had brought yet another pile of papers to add to those which stood stacked on Leo's floor next to his desk. Leo crossed the room to unburden her.

'Why didn't you tell Paul to bring these up?' he asked.

'He's at lunch, and you said you wanted them soon as they came in from Fisher's.' She watched as Leo flicked through the first few pages and shook her pretty, curly head in disdain. 'You oughtn't to be working through lunch on a day like this, Mr Davies. It's lovely outside. You want to get something to eat and have a walk. Do you good. You're looking peaky.' She paused, seeming to scrutinise him more closely. 'How's your love life?'

The enquiry was one which Leo and Felicity regularly made of one another. This offhand intimacy was one of the facets of his relationship with his clerk which Leo particularly enjoyed.

'Not bad, thanks.'

'Boy or girl?'

'Girl, as it happens. A model, rather lovely.'

'Mmm. You like them skinny. Me, I like something I can grab hold of. Not that there's been much grabbing lately.'

'I'm sorry to hear that.'

'Don't worry – it's a lifestyle choice. Thought I'd give men a rest for a few months. Bit of celibacy's good for you now and then – like a detox.'

'I think you mean chastity.'

'Yeah, whatever. Anyway, I'm right off relationships – especially with people round here,' she added meaningfully, referring to an unwise liaison some months previously with a fellow clerk, which had ended badly.

'A very wise decision, Felicity. I came to the same conclusion myself not so long ago.' For Leo, too, against his better judgment, had been known to conduct discreet affairs within chambers, with unfortunate results. 'We have more than a little in common, you and I.'

Felicity looked at her watch. 'Too true. I'm off to get some lunch – you should and all. Don't forget Brian Bennett from Freshfields is coming in at three with Sir Dudley Humble.'

'Bugger – so he is. Thanks for reminding me.' Leo glanced up and winked at her. 'Don't worry. I'll get some lunch.'

Felicity left, reflecting on what a real sweetie Mr Davies was. She passed Jeremy Vane puffing up the staircase – the QC, on his way back from court, looking hot and pink in his bands and courtroom attire, a bundle of papers under his arm.

''Lo, Mr Vane,' said Felicity brightly. 'Lovely day!'

Jeremy muttered some ill-tempered acknowledgement of her greeting and carried on up to his room. Fat tosser, thought Felicity. Like a few others in chambers whose names she could mention – patronising, toffee-nosed, public-school-and-Oxbridge-educated gits – he treated the clerks with the utmost condescension, as though his living didn't depend on them. Not like Leo, who didn't share the illusion that a privileged upbringing somehow conferred social and intellectual superiority. He understood and got on with people like Felicity, and the other clerks, because he didn't think himself any better than they were – just luckier.

A grammar-school boy from Wales, Leo Davies had worked his way to the top of his profession through a combination of brilliance and grinding application. Such tastes as he had acquired along the way – a penchant for expensive cars and clothing, and a passion for collecting pieces of modern art – were real and unaffected, and perhaps because of his lack of pretension he was entirely fearless, in court and out of it. The one weakness in his otherwise robust character – and Leo himself, having no regard for moral conventions, considered it a susceptibility rather than a weakness – was his sexual ambivalence, for he found men just as attractive as women. His past was littered with casual affairs with both sexes, and although he had always endeavoured to be as discreet as possible, the consequences had occasionally proved dire. He had often promised himself that he would mend his ways – for the sake of his infant son, Oliver, if for no one else – but temptation invariably proved irresistible. As a philanderer, Leo was far from heartless. He could be ruthless in his manipulation of lovers for his own ends, as testified by his short-lived marriage, but he found emotional entanglements exhausting, and had this past year vowed to indulge only in the most meaningless and light-hearted relationships. Hence his recent dalliance with Anthea Grieves-Brown, whose vacuity and beauty he found both refreshing and undemanding. He thought of her as he slipped on his jacket and left his room to go in search of lunch. It was a Friday, and although they had made no arrangement to meet, he decided he would call her later and suggest dinner.

3

The conference with Sir Dudley Humble lasted a little over two hours, and was trying for a number of reasons, not least of which was that Sir Dudley was an intractable individual, an ex-army man with a strong controlling streak which made it difficult for him to surrender the management of his affairs, including his legal ones, to others. He had built up Humble Construction Services from scratch, and had earned his knighthood, and a couple of lucrative government contracts into the bargain, through his military connections and in the time-honoured tradition of extending discreet but generous donations to the governing political party of the day. He sat at the other side of the conference table in Leo's room, a tall, square-faced man with shrewd eyes and grizzled white hair and eyebrows, and listened closely as Leo brought him up to date on progress. The case itself was, from Leo's point of view, dreary enough. Three years ago Humble Construction Services had contracted to build an aluminium smelting plant in the Ukraine, and a row had broken out with one of the sub-contractors, with the result that Humble Construction were now suing for breach of contract.

Leo went through the niceties of the contract at some length – often interrupted by terse observations from Sir Dudley – and then set out the arguments of the respective parties as he saw them. Here it was that the problems began. For an intelligent man, Sir Dudley seemed to have peculiar difficulty in listening dispassionately to his lawyer rehearsing the arguments of his opponents.

'I didn't come here to listen to you telling me the other side have a good case, Mr Davies – quite the opposite!'

'Sir Dudley, I'm merely trying to approach the matter realistically. I wouldn't be doing my job if I didn't explore fully the respective strengths and weaknesses of both sides' arguments. Forgive me if, in so doing, I occasionally seem to stray into their territory. I have to do so to maintain a proper perspective. I'm on your side.' Leo's smile was charming and entirely without condescension. 'That's why we're both here.'

Sir Dudley, slightly mollified, tried to contain his impatience, but the conference grew laborious. Sir Dudley felt he understood the rights and wrongs of the case better than anyone else, and found it difficult to accept Leo's advice with any humility. In the end Leo did what he always did with clients of similar intransigence – he held his peace and listened as Sir Dudley told him how to run the case, while he made up his own mind on the issues.

Sir Dudley departed at the end of the meeting with his vanity satisfied, and a sense that he was in control of matters. Leo felt merely wearied by the difficult and somewhat confrontational nature of the afternoon's business, and by the knowledge that there would be more such conferences throughout the duration of the case. Not for the first time that week, he found himself wondering if it was all really worth it. Perhaps in his younger days he had possessed some kind of immunity to vexatious clients, but these days he found people like Sir Dudley extremely tiresome.

I'm getting old, thought Leo. If it weren't for the mortgage on the Chelsea house and Oliver's education.... he'd what? Pack it all in? Hardly. Work was his existence. It was his world, his meat and drink. Everything else was a mere diversion. He was probably just feeling jaded because he'd taken on so much lately. Time for a bit of relaxation. There were papers to read on a new re-insurance case, but they could wait till Monday.

Leo took his mobile from his pocket and tapped in Anthea's number, but it went straight to voicemail. He left a message suggesting dinner. After sending a couple of emails to solicitors, he put his papers together and left chambers. He walked through

Cloisters and down the cobbled slope of King's Bench Walk to where his car was parked, and ten minutes later his Aston Martin was weaving its slow way through the early evening traffic towards Chelsea.

When Anthea picked up Leo's voicemail message, the urge to call him back and agree to meet him was almost irresistible. Despite what she'd said to Lolly, she was a little in love with him. But that was just the point. If she made herself available every time he wanted to see her, he'd lose interest. Men like Leo preferred to make the running, and maintaining uncertainty and unpredictability in an affair was an art. She mustn't make herself too hard to pin down, or he might get bored – just elusive enough to keep things tantalising and hot. She gave a little anguished sigh, trying not to think of what she was missing, and focused on the most effective response. She could text him to say she was busy. Or she could just stay silent.

In the end she opted for the latter as being cooler, and switched off her phone for the rest of the evening so that she didn't have to face the temptation of a further call from him. For Anthea, this was indeed a sacrifice – the first of many she was prepared to make to hold the attention of Leo Davies. In the long run, she was sure it would be worth it.

Leo's house stood in a quiet Chelsea crescent, in the expensive hinterland between Cheyne Walk and the King's Road. With five bedrooms, it was too big to meet the requirements of a single man, but he had bought it at a time when he was entertaining serious thoughts of settling down with his then girlfriend. That relationship had, like so many, met its demise through Leo's unfaithfulness, and looking back, Leo wondered how he could ever have seriously believed in its long-term future. He wasn't the marrying type. He'd tried it once – largely to ward off rumours regarding his libidinous lifestyle which might have stood in the way of his taking silk – and the only good thing to have come out of the whole, sad business was Oliver, his son.

He thought of Oliver now as he mixed himself a drink in the kitchen. He unlocked and slid back the long glass door which led outside. The smooth flagstones of the kitchen floor continued out to a large patio, shaded by a mulberry tree, and beyond this stretched the garden. At the end, delivered and erected just three days ago, stood a new wooden playhouse with a climbing frame and swing attached. Leo smiled and sipped his Scotch as he imagined Oliver's delight when he arrived tomorrow afternoon. He imagined, too, the frozen disapproval of Rachel, Oliver's mother – she would probably consider the climbing frame too advanced and dangerous for a four-year-old. The patterns of their relations now were familiar. Leo would fight down the urge to snap at her, and attempt instead to say something placatory, and Oliver would disregard them both and tear across the lawn to his new plaything with squeals of pleasure.

Leo glanced at his watch. It was only six o'clock. Normally he would have been content, at the end of a gruelling week, with his own company, a light supper and a little television, or possibly a book and some music, but this evening he felt restive. He was just about to call Anthea again, when his mobile rang in his pocket. He pulled it out to answer it, expecting to see Anthea's name on the screen, but saw another instead. Leo felt a little start of pleasure.

'Luca! Where are you?'

'In London.' Luca's suave Italian voice held the same glad note as Leo's. 'I flew in yesterday. I have a flight booked back to Milan tonight, but I don't have to catch it. I thought if you were free this evening we could...' He paused eloquently. '...meet up?'

'Come over,' said Leo without hesitation. 'I'm at home.' He and Luca, a thirty-six year-old Milanese lawyer with whom he worked on a number of cases, had evolved what for Leo was the perfect relationship. Luca came to London on business at least twice a year, and Leo had occasion to fly to Italy now and then on cases. They always made a point of meeting.

A little before seven o'clock he and Luca were sitting drinking and chatting in the garden in the early evening sunshine. Later, while Luca set the table beneath the mulberry tree and laid out candles and glasses, Leo cooked supper. Luca told Leo about the pieces of antique furniture which he had bought for his mother that afternoon at Sotheby's. Leo opened a second bottle of wine and they talked about art, and music, and a little about cases they had, and afterwards, while moths flitted and bumped in the guttering light of the candles, they went upstairs and made love in Leo's big bed. Tomorrow Luca would catch his flight back to Milan. It was an ideal, uncomplicated arrangement for both of them.

A mile away in Fulham Anthea lay stretched out on her sofa, the TV on low, a glass of wine in her hand, bored, but full of hope that her strategy was working. She bet that Leo was thinking about her right now.

4

Rachel arrived at lunchtime the following day, bringing Oliver and his belongings for his weekend stay with his father. She was dressed in a blue cotton blouse and white capri pants, and her dark hair was tied back. At thirty-two, Rachel had pale, smooth skin which never tanned, pretty, sharply-defined features and dark eyes, and a reserved, poised manner. This cool composure, touched with vulnerability, had once been a challenge to Leo – reducing her maidenly modesty to a state of helpless, trembling passion had always been a particular pleasure. But in the last few difficult years the fragility in her personality which had once touched him now seemed to have disappeared. Perhaps he was to blame for that.

In the middle of a hug from his father, Oliver spotted the new playhouse and struggled free to race up the garden towards it. Rachel, who had been covertly looking round for evidence of the existence of a new lover in Leo's life – something she always did on these visits, and not without justification – glanced after him.

Leo watched her face, anticipating disapproval, but none came. 'That looks like fun,' she said somewhat flatly.

'Coffee?' asked Leo.

'Yes, please,' called Rachel over her shoulder as she went out to the garden.

Leo made two cups and took them outside.

'Must have been expensive,' remarked Rachel, nodding towards the playhouse.

'Not especially. Well, not in the scheme of things.'

'The scheme being?' Rachel sat at the table beneath the mulberry tree and gave him a challenging little look. Leo found her arch way of picking him up on meaningless phrases immensely irritating. It was a form of verbal fencing. Why did she do it? To maintain some form of emotional rapport, he supposed. There was something sad about it, this need to engage with him in a mildly aggressive way whenever they met.

'The scheme being,' said Leo, sitting down in the shade, 'to keep my son happy and busy. To bring him up, to educate him, to contribute to his well-being. Our joint project,' he added.

Rachel glanced to where Oliver was struggling, and not quite succeeding, to master the climbing frame. 'It's a bit big for him.'

'It has to be, to give him any fun. Don't want him outgrowing it too fast.' Leo sipped his coffee and glanced at the flat, wasted puddles of wax in the glass storm lanterns from last night. Luca would be catching his flight about now. Next to one of the storm lanterns lay an empty Italian cigarette packet. 'To tell you the truth – ' Even this commonplace phrase brought a small, cynical smile from Rachel, which he tried to ignore. ' – I had the idea you might not approve of it. The climbing frame, I mean.'

'I don't disapprove of the things you do for Oliver.' She caught sight of the cigarette packet and picked it up. 'Just certain aspects of your life. Taken to smoking Italian cigarettes now?'

'They belong to a friend.'

'Who was here not so long ago?'

'That's right.' Leo gave an impatient sigh and glanced to the end of the garden, where Oliver was shouting, 'Mummy, mummy! Watch me!' Rachel smiled and waved. 'So,' asked Leo, amazed that he should allow himself to enter into this sniping contest, but unable to resist, 'still seeing Anthony?'

Rachel's eyes flickered away from Oliver; she paused, and took a slow sip of her coffee. 'No. That's pretty much over.' Anthony was a young barrister at 5 Caper Court, an erstwhile protege of Leo's, whom Rachel had begun seeing last summer.

'I'm sorry to hear that.'

'Why?' Rachel's response was sharp and swift. 'You hated me seeing him. You'd rather have him to yourself.'

'Nonsense. I care about your happiness.'

'That's a laugh.' She drained her coffee cup, then went to the end of the garden to give Oliver a farewell hug. 'By the way,' she said when she came back, 'Oliver's starting at his new prep school a week on Monday.'

Leo was astounded. 'You arranged this without consulting me?'

Rachel shrugged. 'I decided he'd outgrown nursery school. I found an excellent place for him in Chiswick – Kingswood House. I was lucky to get a place so late in the day. Usually it's over-subscribed.'

'I can't believe you did this without speaking to me first. What makes you think I want him going to one of those poncey little places, anyway?'

'Oh, Leo, please – don't tell me you want him going to the local state school.'

Leo had to fight down his anger. 'I'd like to have a say. He's my son. And why does it have to be in Chiswick?'

'It's where he lives. With me.'

'I mean, couldn't you have found somewhere round here? That way I could pick him up occasionally, have him to stay overnight, take him in the next day.'

'Do you know how hellish the traffic is between Chiswick and here in the mornings?'

'You have to come in this direction on your way to work. You don't have to drive.' Leo could see this conversation going nowhere. He didn't know why he was having it.

Rachel picked up her bag. 'It's done now. I'm sorry. Perhaps I should have mentioned it to you.' She fished out her car keys and went through the house to the front door. Leo followed her.

'It's a bit late for the start of the autumn term, isn't it?' he remarked, opening the door for her.

'You know how it is with private schools – short terms, large fees.' Rachel turned to him. 'Can you bring him back by seven tomorrow?' Leo nodded. 'And I take it that your Italian friend – whoever he or she is – won't be on the premises while Oliver's here?'

Leo held the door open. 'Goodbye, Rachel.' She left without another word, and Leo went back to the garden to play with Oliver.

In the car Rachel leant her head against the steering wheel and closed her eyes. Whenever she and Leo met, things never seemed to go the way she meant them to. She wanted to appear relaxed and carefree, as though seeing him was no big deal – but Leo would always be a big deal, damn him, and her attempts at nonchalance merely translated as defensiveness. She'd intended to deliver the news about Ollie's new school in a brightly casual fashion – even though she knew she should have consulted Leo first – but instead she'd merely sounded offhand. It was because of that stupid cigarette packet, and the stupid knowledge that Leo had someone else in his life. He always had someone else. She couldn't help the jealousy seeping through and lacing her words with bitterness. Fool, fool, fool, she told herself. Get over it. If you don't, it's going to poison every relationship in your life. He's a bastard and he always will be.

Rachel didn't need to persuade herself. She, better than anyone, knew all the worst things about Leo. And still she loved him.

5

On Monday morning Michael Gibbon was standing in the middle of the clerks' room, perusing the pages of *The Guardian* and creating something of an obstruction. Bloody hell, thought Felicity, as she tried to edge past him with a tray of coffee cups – he was like a daddy-long-legs, all spindly arms and legs. She administered an admonitory little jog with her elbow and he glanced up, giving her an owlish, apologetic look through his glasses.

'Sorry,' he murmured, and moved nearer the door, thinking he was out of everyone's way – until Leo came through the door seconds later. Leo stared at Michael trying to disentangle the newspaper from his glasses.

'Why on earth,' he asked, 'are you lying in wait behind the door?'

'I was actually trying to read this article,' said Michael, straightening the newspaper. 'It might interest you – Sir Dudley Humble's one of your clients, isn't he?'

'That's right – he's got a contractual dispute with the Ukrainian government over a gas pipeline. Why?'

Michael handed the paper to Leo. The headline of the article read 'Cash For Honours Enquiry Stepped Up', and had a small picture of Sir Dudley next to it. Leo took the paper from Michael and read the opening paragraph.

'*Detectives investigating the cash for honours scandal yesterday interviewed the construction magnate Sir Dudley Humble in relation to a £1 million loan to the Labour party in the run-up to the last election. Sir Dudley said he was 'dismayed' by the suggestion that he had been offered any inducement in return for the loan. 'I have done nothing wrong and have absolutely nothing to hide,' said Sir Dudley. 'It was a straightforward commercial loan to assist the Labour party with their cash flow.' Sir Dudley said he had fully expected the loan to be repaid.'*

'Interesting,' said Leo, skimming the remaining paragraphs. 'But not surprising. One has the impression of a man on the make.'

'What's his background?'

'Ex-military, Falklands veteran – I think he may have been something to do with special operations. He went into construction when he left the army back in the early nineties. He's done pretty well for himself, but his company's run into financial difficulties lately. I reckon he's running this case to scrape up every last penny he can. He fancies himself as a shrewd operator, but I have the feeling – ' He handed the paper back to Michael. ' – that he may have bitten off more than he can chew with the Ukrainians. They're a dodgy bunch, to say the least.'

Henry, the senior clerk, came over in his shirtsleeves bearing a pile of faxes and started to hand them out. Although only thirty six, Henry's sparse hair and expression of melancholy resignation made gave him an air of careworn middle age. 'That's for you, Mr Gibbon...and you, Mr Davies...' Henry glanced across as a tall, dark, young man came into the clerks' room. 'Here you go, Mr Cross, this lot's yours. A weekend's worth.'

'Thank you, Henry.' Anthony began to sift through the faxes. Michael disappeared with his newspaper, and Leo, after a moment's hesitation, came over to speak to Anthony.

'I saw Rachel at the weekend.'

Anthony continued to read, almost as though he hadn't heard, then gave Leo a hostile look. 'And?'

Leo sighed inwardly. For months now, ever since Anthony had begun seeing Rachel, relations between the two men had been strained. Now that they appeared to have broken up, it seemed sensible to Leo that they should try regain some of the lost ground in their friendship.

'She tells me you're not seeing one another any more.'

'Her decision, not mine,' said Anthony curtly. He glanced at his watch. 'Look, if you don't mind, I have to be in court in an hour, and I've got a few things to do – '

'Anthony,' said Leo gently, 'I'm not the enemy. Whatever has happened between you two, it's nothing to do with me.'

'How very true.'

'So – how about a drink later this evening? It seems a long time since we spent any time together.'

Anthony took a deep breath. His offhand manner was entirely at odds with the way he felt. He hated feeling any kind of estrangement from Leo, but all these months while he had been seeing Leo's ex-wife, the idea of behaving towards him with ease and familiarity seemed unnatural, weird. In the distant days when he'd first started as a pupil at Caper Court, Leo had been his mentor and his idol. He'd been entirely captivated by Leo's charismatic personality, his good looks, charm and professional brilliance – it had been a kind of youthful infatuation. He used to listen for Leo's laughter and voice around chambers, or his footstep on the stair – the very air in a room seemed to brighten when Leo came into it – and had been thrilled when Leo had taken him under his wing and helped to gain his tenancy at 5 Caper Court. The discovery, however, that Leo was prepared to express his own fondness for Anthony in ways that were more than merely avuncular had led to confusion. To this day, he was darkly perplexed by his own feelings for Leo. He only knew that he didn't want this tension between them to continue.

He glanced hesitantly at Leo, who was smiling at him as though he knew exactly what was going on in Anthony's heart and head. Leo could still make him feel like an awkward boy, even at twenty seven.

'Fine. Okay.'

'Good,' said Leo. 'I'll come by your room around six.'

Leo went upstairs and sat down at his desk. He surveyed with a heavy heart the memos, reports and documents to which he would have to attend before getting down to his own work. Every aspect of chambers' business was overseen by a separate committee – the finance committee, the pupillage committee, the management committee, the committee to decide how many loo rolls and tea bags they should buy... Really, he could do without it all. Still, as head of chambers, it was his responsibility. He cast a glance over the billing figures for the month and noticed that Maurice Faber's figures were down for the third month in succession. Faber, a thirty-eight year-old barrister who had joined 5 Caper Court when they had merged with another set a few months earlier, and who had been Leo's rival for the position of head of chambers, was regarded as a high-flier with a healthy practice. Oh well, thought Leo – everyone's practice went through lean patches now and then – no doubt Maurice's would pick up again soon. He turned with a sigh to the latest finance report.

By the time six o'clock came, Leo was ready for his drink with Anthony. He had worked without a break all day, and even with the sash window flung wide open and a fan churning the sluggish air, the stifling summer heat made his room muggy and unpleasant. There had been murmurings from several members of chambers recently about the need for air-conditioning, but Leo was pretty sure that the Inns of Court wouldn't look favourably on the introduction of such systems into the fabric of their ancient buildings – a view with which he largely agreed, though a day such as today did make him wonder.

He made a few more notes for the draft opinion on Sir Dudley Humble's case, slipped on his jacket, and went upstairs to Anthony's room. He knocked lightly, and Anthony's voice murmured to him to come in.

Anthony was sprawled behind his desk reading a brief, his sleeves rolled up, tie off and shirt unbuttoned at the neck, the window wide open behind him.

'Won't be a sec,' said Anthony, without lifting his eyes from the page. Leo paced the room idly, glancing with pleasure at Anthony's strong, handsome face, which presently wore a deep frown of concentration. He ran one hand distractedly through his dark hair as he read, then gave a sigh and dropped the papers on his desk. 'Enough of Greek shipowners and their speed and consumption claims.'

'Ready for that drink?'

Anthony nodded, and his dark eyes met Leo's; he smiled and got up, reaching for jacket and tie.

The two men left chambers and strolled down to Middle Temple bar. In the third week of August many of the occupants of the Temple were still on holiday, and without the crowds of law students downing cheap drinks and filling the air with their rowdy chatter, the place had a somewhat abandoned air. Only a handful of people lounged around, reading the papers, or playing quiet games of chess or bridge. Leo bought drinks and he and Anthony went out to the garden. The neatly clipped lawns, the tidy gravel walks and the scent of the rose bushes filled Leo with a sense of repose. There was something supremely soothing about surroundings which had remained largely unchanged down the long decades, and which had seen the passage of so much history. He and Anthony found a secluded bench in a corner of the garden and sipped their drinks, gazing at the late afternoon light gilding the buildings and the lofty plane trees.

There was silence between them for a few moments, the untouched subject of Rachel creating a slight unease. Then Anthony said, 'Look, I know I've been a bit offhand these past few months. It's just – well, Rachel and everything – '

'No need to explain,' said Leo quickly. 'I imagine it's been awkward for you.'

'It has. I mean, she's your ex-wife.' He paused, then leaned forward and said earnestly, as though seeking to unburden himself, 'I think I felt a bit guilty. God knows why.'

'God knows why indeed. Rachel and I were over a long time ago. The relationship was a mistake from the start.'

'You can't regret it entirely – there's Oliver. He's a fantastic little chap.'

'He's the good part. But the rest – ' Leo took a sip of his drink and met Anthony's gaze. 'To be honest, I was pleased when you started seeing her. She needs someone. I'm just sorry it didn't work out.' Anthony looked away, nursing his drink and saying nothing, staring down at the grass. 'You don't have to talk about it if you don't want to, but I'm curious to know what went wrong. You seemed well-suited.'

Anthony sighed. 'It was great at first. You know how things are in the beginning, when you're just getting to know someone, and you think you have plenty in common, you want to be together all the time... That's how it was. But after a while, when the initial glow had worn off, she became restless. Difficult, even. I'm sure it was just as much my fault... Anyway, we argued a lot. I began to realise – ' Anthony took a reflective swallow of his drink. ' – that she's not an easy woman to be around. In fact, I think she's got issues, as the shrinks say.'

Leo nodded. 'Difficult childhood. She's never really liked men, I don't think.'

'That's where you're wrong.' Anthony turned his gaze on Leo. 'Certainly as regards one particular man. You. I think she's still in love with you.'

'I hope not.'

'No,' agreed Anthony with a wry smile. 'Not good for her. Not good for anyone.'

Including me, thought Anthony. He looked away from Leo, staring at his glass as he let his unspoken thoughts unwind in his head. He was glad to be here, glad to have Leo to himself once more. Any relationship which put distance between himself and Leo had to be a mistake. The strength of his own feelings, appropriate or otherwise, didn't matter. No one needed to know. Just so long as he could see and be with Leo, the way it always used to be.

'In that regard,' said Leo, 'and considering all the mistakes I've made, I'm quite determined never to become emotionally entangled in anyone's life again.' He drained his glass. 'Never, ever.'

'You said that as though you meant it. But I can't honestly imagine you leading a monkish existence.'

'Who said anything about that? I was talking about emotional involvement, remember. I'm presently seeing a young woman, with whom my relationship is as relentlessly superficial as she is, and we're both quite content. As a matter of fact – ' Leo glanced at his watch, ' – I was thinking of going round to see her this evening. She hasn't been answering my calls.'

'That must be something of a novelty for you.'

'It is. She's only twenty eight, so perhaps she's decided I'm too old and boring to bother with.'

'I somehow doubt it. Self-deprecation doesn't become you, by the way. It's most unconvincing. Time for another drink?'

Leo smiled. It was a pleasure to have resumed the easy intimacy of his friendship with Anthony. 'Oh, I think so.'

6

Lucy Wavell kicked off her ballet pumps, slung her A-level art portfolio and her schoolbag on to the sofa, and wandered into Anthea's kitchen to forage for food. She was starving. She'd had no lunch because the queue in the lunch hall had been ginormous – all those new kids just didn't know the protocol – and she had to get to the auditions for the school play on time, though to be honest she only went along because the lovely Angus, with the floppy blond hair and drawling voice, was probably going to be in it. She gazed into the fridge, pulled out a half-eaten tub of taramasalata, the remnants of a wholemeal loaf, and a bottle of vodka. She stuck two slices of bread into the toaster and held the bottle up. Three-quarters full. Ant would never notice if she nicked some. What was the point of having a half-sister who was a model and had her own place in Fulham if you couldn't nick her drink and borrow her clothes?

She poured herself a generous measure of Smirnoff Blue Label and topped it off with some orange juice, then wandered through to the bathroom to inspect the cabinet for interesting pills. Last time she'd found some Valium. Seeing a bottle of Nembutal, she shook a few out into her palm and pocketed them. Then she went back to the kitchen, cut her toast into fingers, and took it with the tub of taramasalata and the tumbler of vodka and orange through to the living room. She stretched out on the sofa, clicked on the TV with the remote, and flicked her way through the music channels as she ate.

After a while she got up, put the plate and glass on one side, brushed the crumbs from the lap of her tiny skirt, and strolled to the window. She opened it wide and leaned far out into the evening sunshine, enjoying the breeze in her hair and the buzz from the vodka, letting her thoughts drift idly from boys to parties to clothes and back to boys again as she watched the commuters making their way home from work.

A smart, dark blue car came round the corner and cruised the street slowly, looking for a parking space. Lucy watched as the car skillfully negotiated a space between a motor bike and a Nissan. She wished she could get the hang of reverse parking. She was so crap at it. Her driving instructor kept giving her what he thought were these useful little guidelines involving the mirror and the kerb, but they never worked for her. From here Lucy's thoughts drifted like tumbleweed to the matter of her driving test, and how brilliant it would be when she got her licence and could drive to school, instead of catching the manky coach every day.

A man got out of the car, and Lucy studied him with interest. He looked quite fit, in spite of that silver hair. Good-looking, definitely. She watched as he strolled round the car to the pavement. He was heading here, towards the house. Maybe he lived in the flat below. He disappeared from view, and she was just about to let him slip from her thoughts, when the intercom buzzed, startling her. She padded across and pressed the button, and said, 'Hello?'

'Anthea?' The man's voice was moderately deep, and rather nice.

Lucy smiled, said nothing, and pressed the buzzer to open the main door. Then she waited.

Leo came upstairs and knocked lightly on the door of Anthea's flat. He was surprised when it was opened by a pretty, barefoot girl, much smaller than leggy Anthea, dressed in a cropped T-shirt and a tiny ruffled skirt, and with tangled, shoulder-length dark hair and smokily made-up eyes. She smiled at him sweetly.

'Anthea's not in, I'm afraid, but she shouldn't be long. Would you like to wait?' She turned away without waiting for a reply.

Bemused, Leo closed the door and followed her into the living room.

'Drink?' asked the girl. 'We've got some lovely vodka.' She gave him another poised little smile.

Leo returned the smile. 'If it's lovely, I'd better have some.'

Lucy went through to the kitchen and returned with the bottle of Smirnoff and two glasses with ice in them. She sloshed liberal amounts of vodka into both and handed one to Leo.

'Thanks. I'm Leo Davies, by the way.'

Lucy chinked her glass against his. 'Hello, Leo.'

'And you are..?'

'Lucy, Anthea's sister.' She took a swig of her vodka.

Leo looked uncertainly at his. 'You wouldn't have tonic, by any chance?'

'I don't think so.'

Lucy took her drink over to the sofa and curled up on it in what she hoped was a sophisticated but provocative manner. She desperately wanted to make an impression on this divine man with the killer smile and crazy blue eyes. He might be middle-aged, but he was a lot better than the usual divs Anthea went out with. He actually had a bit of style. A little thrill ran through her as she wondered what it would be like to be kissed by someone that old. He looked like he would know what he was doing.

While these untoward thoughts ran through her mind, Leo sat down in an armchair, a little nonplussed by the sexy creature opposite, with her childlike face and seductive expression.

'So,' he asked, glancing at the art portfolio and bag of books, 'do you go to school?'

'Oh no,' said Lucy quickly, and took a sip of her vodka. 'I'm at college. I'm a fashion student.'

'I see.' Leo glanced again at the inch-and-a-half of neat vodka in his glass, which he had no intention of drinking.

'What do you do?' asked Lucy, dark eyes fastened on his.

'I'm a barrister,' replied Leo.

'Cool.'

A long silence followed. Leo, usually adept at making small talk with women, was feeling strangely out of his depth. Lucy's inscrutable gaze was fastened on his face. He had no idea what she was thinking. In fact, Lucy was busy weighing up the possibilities. She'd never realised it was possible to fancy anyone over thirty. She'd certainly never been interested in any of Anthea's men before, because they were usually complete cretins – but this man was different, though she couldn't say why.

'I like your car,' she said at last.

'Do you?' said Leo, realising she must have watched him arrive, and beginning to feel like a character in a French film.

'What make is it?'

Leo noticed with surprise that she'd nearly finished her drink. How old could she be? Nineteen or twenty, he supposed, if she was at college. 'An Aston Martin,' he replied.

'Wicked.'

'You know,' said Leo, glancing at his watch, 'I really don't want to impose on you. Perhaps Anthea's – '

'Don't worry.' Lucy waved a hand. 'She'll be back any minute.' There was another long pause. 'Actually,' said Lucy, who was feeling quite pleasantly pissed, 'she's not really my sister. She's my half sister. My mother married Anthea's dad, and had Anthea, then divorced him, then she married *my* dad, and had me, and then she divorced *my* dad – ' She stopped and sighed.

Leo didn't really see a way to pick up this thread of conversation and take it anywhere, so he set down his glass. 'I'd better go,' he said. 'Tell Anthea I'll call her later.' He stood up.

Lucy stayed where she was, jiggling her empty glass and winding a strand of hair round one finger. 'OK. Nice to meet you, Leo.'

Leo found himself smiling as he went back downstairs to his car. A very pretty, if somewhat peculiar, young lady.

Lucy realised she shouldn't have drunk all that vodka, not on top of the toast and taramasalata. She didn't feel good. Not good at all. She went through to the bathroom, stuck two fingers down her throat, and made herself sick. She inspected the gooey rainbow mixture of orange and pink, then flushed the loo, wiped her mouth, and went to make herself some coffee.

Fifteen minutes later Anthea arrived back. She'd been at a photo shoot all afternoon and was tired and hot.

'What are you doing here?' she asked Lucy, somewhat unkindly.

'Forgot my house keys. Mum's not back till late. I thought you wouldn't mind if I came round here.'

'Well, I do mind.' She saw Leo's discarded drink sitting on a side table. 'Have you been at my vodka again?'

Lucy yawned. 'I made a drink for one of your friends. I don't think he liked it.'

Anthea picked up the glass to take it to the kitchen. 'Get your feet off the sofa. What friend?'

'*God,* stop being so stressy – I haven't even got shoes on. Leo something.'

Anthea stopped in the doorway. 'Leo Davies? He came round here?'

Lucy made a mock-dumb face at her sister. 'Like – *yeah.*'

Anthea smiled, surprised and pleased. She went to the kitchen and rinsed the glass, put the cap back on the vodka and returned it to the fridge. Not answering his calls or his messages appeared to have had an effect. She went back through to the living room.

'So, what did he say?'

'Oh – we had a bit of a chat about this and that,' said Lucy nonchalantly, 'then he said he had to go.'

'Nothing else?'

'Just that he'd ring later.' Lucy caught Anthea's pleased little smile. 'Aren't you pissed off that you missed him? I would be. He's really buff.'

Anthea shot her a glance. 'I hope you behaved yourself.'

Lucy smiled sweetly. 'I was the perfect hostess.'

'I'm sure.' Anthea went to a drawer. 'Here – you can take my spare key and go home. I've got stuff to do.'

'OK.'

'I want it back, mind.'

'Yeah, sure.' Lucy slipped on her pumps, picked up her things and headed for the door. She wiggled her fingers at Anthea in

31

farewell. 'Laters.'

When Lucy had gone, Anthea ran a bath and lay soaking, thinking about Leo. Evidently her stalling tactic had worked. He was in hot pursuit. What would she do when he rang later? If she put him off again, she risked sending out the wrong message. Besides, she was desperate – she'd been deliberately blanking the thought of sex with him all weekend, and now she'd allowed herself to think of it, she was absolutely aching for him. She was suddenly touched with apprehension. What if he didn't call after all?

But Leo rang. He rang a little after nine and, cool as she tried to be, Anthea ended up inviting him round.

'I can't stay long,' said Leo when he got there. He took her in his arms and kissed her slowly. 'I have an early start tomorrow.'

'Then let's not hang around,' murmured Anthea, unbuttoning his shirt and kissing his neck. 'I'm already a few steps ahead of you.' She was wearing only a crimson silk robe. Leo loosened the sash and let it fall open, and slipped his hands inside to caress her. She gave an involuntary little shiver of pleasure. She was breaking her own rules. She should probably have held out for another week. But this – the feeling of him, his kiss, the touch of his hands, was too pleasurable. Sex with Leo was like a drug, and she couldn't get enough of it.

7

When Leo woke, it took him a moment or two to realise where he was. The light through the blind cast a blue shadow across the room. He glanced across and saw Anthea, still asleep, her blonde hair tumbled on the pillow. He gave a faint groan and let his head fall back. His mistake had been in agreeing to stay for a drink after their first delirious bout of sex, but pleasuring Anthea was an exhausting business, and he'd needed one. Thereafter, insatiable girl that she was, she'd found innovative and delightful ways to persuade him to stay even longer, and in the end he'd been too tired to get dressed and drive home. He'd probably have been over the limit anyway.

Telling himself he was too old for this kind of thing, Leo eased himself gently out of bed, being careful not to wake Anthea, got dressed, and let himself out of her flat. As he drove the short distance home, still yawning, he was appalled to realise that it was nearly half past nine. The last twelve hours were strewn with the wreckage of good intentions. Yesterday he'd fully intended to spend the evening reading the papers in that re-insurance case. He'd only meant to stop off at Anthea's for half an hour or so beforehand. Even when he arranged to meet her later, he'd promised himself it wouldn't be for long, and that he'd be up early this morning to get into chambers before eight. He edged his way impatiently through the late rush hour traffic, telling himself he only had his own libido to blame.

Henry barely raised an eyebrow when Leo came crashing into the clerks' room an hour later.

'Morning Mr Davies. You're due in court in ten minutes.'

'I bloody well know that, Henry! Have you seen my copy of Schofield anywhere? It's disappeared from my room.'

'Afraid not, sir. Maybe one of the pupils has it.'

Maurice Faber, standing in his shirtsleeves by the photocopier, glanced up.

'Sorry, old man – it's in my room. I borrowed it last night.'

Maurice, a swarthy, keen-eyed man in his early forties, smiled apologetically but without particular sincerity. It was only a year ago that he, together with a rebellious rump of fellow barristers from another set of chambers, had joined 5 Caper Court. A QC of considerable reputation, Maurice at the time had harboured confident ambitions of becoming head of 5 Caper Court, having been responsible for much modernisation and progressive thinking in relation to promoting the image of chambers. Leo, however, had won the chambers' vote by a narrow majority, and although Maurice had accepted his defeat graciously, a certain tension remained between the two men.

At that moment Henry re-appeared bearing a copy of the necessary textbook. 'Here you go,' he said, handing it to Leo with the air of an efficient footman. 'Mr Fry had a copy in his room.'

'God bless you, Henry,' said Leo, rifling through the volume to mark the relevant pages. Then he picked up his robing bag and the remainder of his papers, and hurried off to court.

Maurice Faber finished his photocopying and left the clerks' room a few moments later. Felicity followed his departure with thoughtful eyes. Returning to her computer screen, she brought up the latest billing figures and scrutinised them.

'Don't know how Mr Faber stays so cheerful,' she remarked to Henry. 'His August receipts are well down.'

'That's the third month in a row.'

'You'd've thought he'd look a bit more bothered, but he seems happy as Larry. I wonder why his work's slowing down. What d'you think?'

Henry shrugged. 'Who can say? Ours not to reason why, Fliss.'

Felicity wasn't sure she agreed with this – not so long as she was on a percentage of Maurice Faber's earnings.

Around three that afternoon, Leo wandered over to Inner Temple Common Room for the relaxing ritual of taking tea with fellow members of chambers and other barristers. Leo had helped himself to a cup of tea and some biscuits, and was making his way across the common room to join Michael Gibbon and Roger Fry, when Maurice accosted him, evidently somewhat irate.

'I've just been speaking to Linklaters, Leo. You do realise you've been giving entirely inappropriate advice?'

'Sorry, Maurice – what are you talking about?'

'I'm talking about that anti-suit injunction I obtained last spring. I gather you've been giving your Australian clients advice as to how they can avoid the effects of it.'

'Perhaps you shouldn't have sought an injunction in such wide terms,' replied Leo. 'Notoriously tricky, these jurisdiction points, aren't they? Sorry if you've been inconvenienced.'

Leo began to move away, but Maurice grabbed his sleeve, causing tea to splash out of Leo's cup. 'Mind the suit, Maurice,' murmured Leo, setting his teacup down on the table and wiping his sleeve.

'Inconvenienced? It's more than that – what you've done amounts to contempt.'

'Oh, don't be ridiculous. When I gave that advice, I had no idea of the background.'

'You do realise I could take proceedings against you? That might make you less flippant!'

'Careful – he knows a good lawyer!' observed Michael. Roger laughed, but Maurice strode off in high dudgeon.

'What was that about?' asked Roger, as Leo sat down.

'He's got a case where he managed to obtain an injunction in respect of a UK jurisdiction clause. Some Australians came to me recently for advice as to how to get round it, and I gave it. Possibly I went further than I should have done. I wasn't aware of the injunction, to be honest. In hindsight perhaps I should have asked, but I do think these anti-suit injunctions are ridiculous, anyway.' Leo took a sip of his tea. 'I suppose, technically, he could have me done for contempt, though it would hardly make for friendly relations in chambers.'

'I wouldn't put it past him,' said Roger. 'He's such an arrogant sod. It was bad enough when I was his pupil, but lately – ' Roger broke off in exasperation. He was a bespectacled, clever young man with a rumpled aspect, inclined to put matters of the intellect before those of the person. Leo liked him because of his sharp mind and affable disposition, and was surprised by this sudden burst of hostility.

'Maurice Faber's arrogance hardly marks him out from the rest of the Bar. What's brought this on, all of a sudden?'

'You're head of chambers – don't you object when he doesn't pay his rent on time?'

'Mildly,' replied Leo, 'but he's always good for it in the long run. I don't see why the chambers' budget should concern you.'

'I'm just fed up with the way he treats chambers as his personal fiefdom. And you know his receipts are down, don't you?'

'That's hardly your business,' observed Michael.

'Of course it is! It's partly the reason why I'm so fed up with this useless set-up – no one has a proper sense of financial obligation. And the system's utterly moribund. All these bloody committees to decide what kind of coffee we buy...'

Leo gave Roger a thoughtful look. 'Is this about chambers, or about Maurice? Come on, tell me.'

'Both, if you must know, but Maurice mainly.'

'Because he's late with his rent?'

'More than that. He and I had a row a month ago – nothing major, but since then he's been doing every little thing he can to make my life difficult. I'm pretty sure he leaned on Peter to instruct Marcus, rather than me, in that big Preston case recently. And there's something else, to do with Melanie. You remember her?'

Melanie had been a pupil of Maurice's until a month or two ago. She was an attractive girl with a formidable character, and Leo's fondest recollection was of her effectively and robustly rebuffing Maurice's advances at the chambers' Christmas party.

'I certainly remember the incident at the Christmas party. Don't tell me Maurice is still pestering her?'

'No, it's worse than that. She applied for a job recently – a really good one, could have been tailor-made for her. She was so sure she was going to get it. Then at the last moment, they rejected her.'

'And?'

'I'm pretty sure it was because Maurice gave her a bad confidential reference. I mean, you know Melanie – she's bright, capable, reliable. She's got fantastic qualifications. She made it all the way to a final interview. It must have been that bastard Maurice.'

'You don't know that for sure,' observed Michael.

'No, I don't. But I'd love to be able to prove it. He could carry on doing her that kind of damage indefinitely, if he wants to. She can't get anywhere without a reference from him.'

'I think you're possibly being paranoid. He's not that petty,' said Leo.

'Isn't he? I know Maurice better than you do, remember – he and I go back a long way. He bears grudges. He's not going to let you forget about that injunction in a hurry, I promise you.' Roger sighed and glanced at his watch. 'I've got a con in ten minutes. I'd better go.'

'What about your other grievances? The ones to do with chambers?'

'They'll wait for another time.' Roger drained his tea cup and left the common room.

8

Like many seventeen-year-old girls, Lucy Wavell believed that the universe, of which she was the centre, had been specially created for her. Everything in the great, big, wonderful world – every war and famine and pop song and celebrity scandal and political intrigue, each plane crash, earthquake, tsunami and hurricane – existed merely as part of the backdrop to her own unique and wonderful existence. Fulfilment for Lucy was to be found in hanging out with friends from her expensive private school, talking about boys, bitching about other girls, buying clothes, going to the pub, slagging off teachers, and doing a bit of desultory schoolwork now and then. She thought of the future mainly in terms of the next party or King's Road shopping trip, and her chief goal in life was to own a Mulberry 'Roxanne' bag. Although Lucy credited herself with possessing a very individual style, the truth was that she dressed, spoke, thought and acted like every other Sloaney girl in London.

What marked Lucy out was her secret crush. No other girl she knew was secretly in love with a middle-aged man. She'd rather have *died* than confide in even her closest friends, so she had to pretend to have the average infatuations with various boys her age – though privately she now thought that Anthea's lovely Leo made Angus, he of the floppy hair and drawling voice, look sad. So what if Angus's dad had an estate in Scotland? The fact was, *Angus* didn't – all Angus had, apart from his blond hair and his far-back voice, were four dodgy AS levels, a part in the school play, and an arse that looked more than averagely nice in rugby shorts. Leo, on the other hand, was a gorgeous-looking QC who drove an Aston Martin, had a house in Chelsea and another in the country, earned loads of dosh, wore handmade Kilgour suits, collected art, knew all the cool, grown-up places to hang out, and was probably much better at sex than anyone Angus's age.

This much she knew, or had gleaned, from Anthea. The information concerning Leo's academic and professional background she had picked up from the 5 Caper Court website, which she frequently Googled just so she could gaze at the postage-stamp-sized picture of Leo. Although she had no idea what 'specialising in international commercial litigation, insurance and re-insurance, international sales and commodity trading' meant, Lucy thought it sounded *totally* intellectual.

Ever since she'd had a crush on Mr Bishop, her biology teacher in Year 10, Lucy was pretty sure that older men were her thing. Some days she would think of Leo with helpless yearning, convinced he was totally out of her reach, but on other, better days she would persuade herself that any man of his age would totally die to go to bed with someone as young as she was. Well, as young as he probably thought she was, after the fashion student lie. OK, so she hadn't actually been to bed with anyone yet, but that was sort of the point. How fantastic would it be to lose your virginity to someone like Leo? It would probably be a truly seductive, mind-blowing experience, as opposed to having some sweaty , half-drunk sixth former fumble his way into your knickers in the dark at a party.

Much to Anthea's annoyance, Lucy took to going round to Anthea's after school every day that week, in case Leo stopped by again.

'I'm going to take your key away,' she told Lucy, after coming home one evening to find her lying on the sofa eating a bacon sandwich and drinking brandy and lemonade.

'You can't. You know mum wants me to have it as a back-up in case I lose the house key. Anyway, she's out all the time. It gets boring at home. I like coming here.'

'Yes, well you're rather in the way. And I don't like my flat stinking of fry-ups. What on earth is that you're drinking? My God, give it here.'

Lucy finished the last of her sandwich and licked ketchup from her thumb.

'Are you going out with Leo tonight?'

'I am, as it happens. He's picking me up in half an hour. What's it to you?'

'Nothing. I just wondered.' Anthea unpinned her hair and went through to her bedroom. Lucy followed her. 'Ant?'

'What? Look, I'm about to take a shower.'

'Could I stay here this evening?'

'And drink all my booze? No chance.'

'Oh, please. Mum's gone on the Eurostar to Paris for the day, and she won't be back till really late. I hate being in that house on my own.'

'I told you, I'm going out myself. What's the difference?'

'It's just nicer here.'

'No.'

'Well, can I stay till you go out?'

Anthea shrugged. 'I suppose so. Now, let me get my shower.'

Lucy went back to the living room and settled herself in front of the television. In just thirty minutes she would be seeing Leo. With this thought, she dived into the large, grubby bag she used to carry her books and rummaged for her Juicy Tube and a mirror. When she had slicked her mouth to pouting, glossy perfection, she mussed her hair artfully with one hand while squinting in her tiny hand mirror to examine the effect. Then she chucked the things back in her bag and lay back with a sigh of anticipation.

Anthea was still putting on her make-up when Leo arrived. Hearing the buzzer, she called out, 'Can you get that, Luce?'

Lucy got up, tugging her Miss Sixty jeans a little lower on her hips, and went to let Leo in. He was dressed in tan trousers and a light blue silk shirt, and expensive-looking shoes, and she could smell the faintest whiff of some divinely subtle cologne. She was so used to thinking of him lately in terms of the black-and-white chambers website picture that it gave her a delicious, tingling shock to see him in the flesh, in living colour, with his silver hair and clean-cut features. He gave Lucy a smile of surprise, and said, 'Hello again.'

'Hi.' Lucy shook back her dark hair in what she hoped was a sexily casual manner. 'Come in. Ant's just getting ready.'

She settled herself on the sofa and gazed up at Leo, who stood in the middle of the room feeling, yet again, somewhat at a loss. This girl had a way of looking at him which was both provocative and unsettling.

'Studies going okay?' he asked.

Lucy nodded. A little fear gripped her heart. She hoped Anthea hadn't told him she was still at school. That would blow everything. It seemed unlikely, though, that Anthea would choose to discuss her younger sister with Leo. 'Fine, thanks. How about you. Any big cases?' God, he was so buff, she could stare at him all evening.

Leo smiled again, bemused. 'One or two.'

Lucy thought of the website, from which she'd learned by heart every tiny particular there was to know about him, including his big recent cases. She'd've loved to chat to him in a really grown-up way about them, but then he'd know she'd been checking out the website. How uncool would that look? She continued to gaze at him thoughtfully, and Leo's eyes couldn't help but be drawn, first to the sheen of her plump, slightly-parted lips, then to her dark, lovely eyes, and lastly to the low, soft expanse of skin revealed by her T-shirt riding up from her hipster jeans. She was, whether she knew it or not, the epitome of smouldering, childlike sexuality. Leo found his thoughts travelling in such a swift, unseemly direction that he was actually relieved when, at that moment, Anthea came into the room. The contrast between Lucy's tousled young sexuality and Anthea's sleek loveliness was not lost on Leo, and he found himself marvelling, not for the first time, at the differing ways and degrees in which women exerted their particular charms.

'Where are you going?' asked Lucy, glancing from Anthea to Leo.

'The Kandinski exhibition,' said Leo.

Anthea gave a little laugh as she checked the contents of her bag. 'OK. Another artist I've never heard of.'

Lucy, who had risen to put on her shoes and pick up her bag, pre-empting the possibility of being bossed around by Anthea, said, 'He's an abstract painter, member of the Bauhaus. It's a good exhibition.'

Anthea gave her sister a waspish look. 'I didn't know you'd been.'

Lucy just stopped herself in time from telling them that she'd been with the school. Instead, she looked at Leo and said, 'I like 'The Cossacks' best. It's a totally amazing picture.'

'I'll look out for it,' said Leo.

They all left together, and on the way downstairs Leo asked Lucy if they could give her a lift.

'She's quite capable of walking,' said Anthea. 'It's only half a mile.'

'I'd love a lift,' said Lucy.

She snuggled into the back of Leo's DB8, and the smell of leather and the sense of cocooned, expensive safety immediately reminded her of her father, and journeys through Italy as a child. She watched Leo's profile as he drove, glancing from time to time at his hands, the wheel slipping beneath his fingers, the firm, easy way he shifted through the gears. He was so, so sexy. She sat in the back of his car and inhaled the very presence of him. She was in love, no question.

It took only five minutes to drive to her mother's house in South Kensington, but for Lucy the ride was pure heaven. She stepped out on to the pavement, and Leo slid the window down.

'Thanks a lot,' said Lucy.

'My pleasure.'

Ohmigod, thought Lucy, the way he looked at her when he said that! She waved goodnight and floated on air to the front door. She didn't care if he was over forty, she didn't care if he belonged to Anthea. He absolutely had to be the first man she went to bed with – no one else would do. It was just a question of working out how, and when.

9

Leo thought about what Roger had told him about Maurice. He didn't seriously believe Roger's suspicions about Melanie's confidential reference, and he wasn't especially concerned about Maurice's finances – what troubled Leo more was the note of general dissatisfaction which Roger had sounded. He had already noticed an air of general restiveness about the junior members of chambers, and that wasn't a healthy thing. Leo liked to run a happy ship. He decided to speak to Anthony about it over lunch.

He went to Anthony's room a little before one and suggested a bite in Middle Temple Hall. For all its antiquity and magnificence the long hall, with its Elizabethan hammerbeam roof and wainscotted walls and elegant glass bay windows, was very much a functional place, and each day, below Van Dyke's imposing equestrian portrait of Charles I, luncheon of a 'school dinners' variety was served to the hungry members of Middle Temple. Leo took his plate of shepherd's pie and mixed veg to one of the long, polished oak tables and sat down opposite Anthony.

'I see you went for the shepherd's pie, too,' he remarked, glancing at Anthony's plate.

'I didn't much care for the look of the macaroni cheese. The apple crumble looks all right – I might have some of that after. I need to fuel up – I'm going drinking with Roger this evening.'

'That's what I wanted to talk to you about. How do you think he is these days?'

'Roger? He's all right, I suppose. Having a bit of a moan, like all of us.'

'A moan about what?'

'Oh, he's got a particular bee in his bonnet about Maurice.

The others are just banging on about the usual things – people not returning books, people ordering couriers on other people's accounts and then not paying for them – the usual paranoia. Rory and Simon are always complaining about how long it takes them to get into chambers each day.'

'It worries me that people are dissatisfied.'

'I wouldn't beat yourself up about it – people like to have something to gripe about. As for the commuting – you're hardly responsible for the state of the roads and the railways.' Anthony scraped up the remains of his shepherd's pie. 'Actually, I'm thinking of getting a motor bike.'

'Really? I thought of that myself once. Anyway, I'll see if there's something that can't be done about making sure books are returned. I find it somewhat irritating myself. I'd be grateful if you'd keep me updated on what feelings are like among the junior tenants – it's not always easy for me to take soundings.'

Anthony grinned. 'This paternalism is quite touching – I've never seen it in you before.'

'Perhaps it's a result of actually being a father.' Leo smiled. 'Oliver's starting his new school next week. I'm trying to persuade Rachel to let me take him on his first day, but she seems to regard that as her privilege.'

'Why don't you both take him?'

'I suppose we could. Or maybe I might pick him up, if I can get away. We'll strike some kind of compromise. We generally do. I have to be careful not to rock the boat, though – the access arrangement we have only exists on her say-so.'

'I think I might grab some pudding,' said Anthony. 'What about you?'

'I'll leave that stuff to fit, young things like you,' said Leo. 'Just a coffee for me, thanks.'

Lucy and her best friend, Georgia, were sitting on the wall outside the school lunch hall, gossiping in the late summer sunshine.

'My God, Phyllida is really, *really* beginning to annoy me,' said Georgia. 'We're sitting in English, right? And she's all like, oh I haven't got my copy of *Hamlet*, can we share? Which is so annoying. And then afterwards she's all like, can I borrow your copy to do my notes? And she doesn't wait for me to say yes or anything, she just sort of takes it, and I'm like – thanks for asking! And then she forgets to give it back to me, so I can't do my homework, and so Mrs Lees is like – '

Lucy stopped Georgia, in mid-flow. 'Shut it. Here she comes.'

Phyllida, flicking back her blonde hair over one shoulder, strolled past Lucy and Georgia. Lucy and Georgia smiled, twinkling their fingers and murmuring, 'Hi, Phil!' They watched her retreating figure with cold, candid eyes, their smiles fading.

'Anyway,' said Lucy, anxious to revert to the subject of Leo, which Georgia had mysteriously hijacked a few minutes ago so that they'd somehow ended up discussing Phyllida Dutton, 'this amazing man I was telling you about – '

'Oh yeah – how old did you say he was?'

Lucy didn't want to confide too many details about Leo – she needed Georgia's help on the 'get-Leo-to-bed' project, but she had to be careful.

'Just older.' She couldn't tell Georgia he was over forty. Georgia would totally freak. 'But honestly, he's like, so totally fit! The trouble is, it's not exactly easy to get him on his own. I need to sort of set it up, right?'

Georgia nodded.

'So this is what you do.' And Lucy proceeded to outline her plan to Georgia.

Later, when school was finished, instead of taking the coach home, Lucy went round to Anthea's and let herself in. She knew Anthea was away on a shoot that day and wouldn't be back till late. This time she left the fridge and the vodka bottle strictly alone. She didn't want Anthea to know she'd been there.

She went to the phone and lifted the handset, scrolling through the numbers in the address book until she found Leo's mobile number. Fishing her own mobile from her bag, she tapped in the number and saved it. Then she wandered into Anthea's room and rummaged through the contents of her teeming wardrobe. Ant had so much good stuff. Pity she was so tall. Still, there were a couple of things that would do. In the end Lucy took away a diaphanous little Chloe top, a black and silver belt, and a pair of precariously beautiful dark red Jimmy Choos, which didn't look like they'd ever been worn. Ant would never miss them. Not for a bit, anyway.

10

'We can take him together.'

'That's silly. It means you have to drive from Chelsea to Chiswick at the height of the rush hour.'

'I don't mind. It's his first day. Besides, I can take the tube to Chiswick and then into the office.' Leo tucked the phone under his chin and reached out for his pen.

'You, on the tube?'

'I'm not wedded to my car, you know.'

'I sometimes wonder. '

'I don't suppose,' said Leo, 'that you'd consider letting Oliver stay overnight with me on Sunday as well as Saturday? That way I could get him ready for school on Monday morning, and we could come over and meet you there.'

'I don't think so.'

Leo sighed. Why had he even bothered suggesting it? She scarcely wanted him there on Oliver's first morning of school as it was. Why? Something to do with wanting to retain control, to keep Oliver to herself. She always made out that she wanted Leo to see as much of Oliver as possible, but he suspected that she begrudged the hours Oliver spent with him. In the past she'd trotted out all kinds of excuses to truncate visits or cancel them altogether, saying it wasn't convenient, that it would be disruptive to Oliver – once, worst of all, that she didn't want Oliver being exposed to the dissolute private life she suspected Leo of leading. That last one had led to a hellish row, and to a crisis of conscience on Leo's part.

'I thought not. Anyway, don't worry about what kind of transport I'm going to take. I'll be there. What time does he start?'

'Quarter to nine.'

'Fine. And Rachel?'

'What?'

'I'd like to get him something – you know, something for school.'

'I think he's got everything he needs.'

'Well, I'll get him a pencil case and some stuff to put it in it, anyway. I'll give it to him at the weekend.'

'Fine.'

'I'll see you on Saturday morning.'

Leo put down the phone and sighed. He'd had a heavy morning in court, and the last thing he needed was Rachel's obstructiveness. She was only like this when she was unhappy, and that probably had a lot to do with Anthony. What the woman needed was some therapeutic sex – Leo was a great believer in its remedial properties – but she was so bloody icy and brittle these days that was unlikely. Well, she was her own problem, and not his any more. He thought briefly, and with light-hearted thankfulness, of lovely Anthea. A girl with no agenda, no axe to grind, no demands to make, except of the most enjoyable kind. A pity she was away this evening – that slender, supple body of hers was just what he needed after a day such as today. He liked, too, the fact that she didn't always make herself available. It somehow heightened his interest.

Leo went to fetch a mug of coffee, and then sat down to read the latest bundle of documents which had come in on the Humble Construction case, and which appeared to consist of yet more invoices for the supply of goods and materials involved in the construction of the smelting plant. Half an hour into his work, Leo came across a document which gave him pause. It was an invoice raised by a London company called Landline for the lining of furnaces at the aluminium plant. Nothing strange in that, except that it seemed to be at odds with another invoice which he recalled seeing earlier on in the case.

Leo went to a row of box files and began to look through them. It took him ten minutes to locate the document he wanted

– an invoice from the Ukrainian sub-contractors, Zobil, for exactly the same work, but for a considerably lower sum. He laid both documents on his desk and studied them, trying to think of a reason for the discrepancy. Eventually he lifted the phone and rang Brian Bennett. He explained what he had found.

'I'm just rather puzzled. Can you think of any reason why there should be two invoices for the same work?'

'Not off-hand,' said Brian. 'To be honest, it escaped my notice. You're obviously more eagle-eyed than I am.'

'The only thing I can think of,' said Leo, inspecting at the invoices, 'is that this furnace lining work which Humble say Zobil didn't complete satisfactorily was subsequently done by the London company, at greater cost. In which case, shouldn't we be increasing our claim?'

'You would think so – but Sir Dudley hasn't mentioned anything about the work being done elsewhere.'

'No. And I don't really see what a London-based company is doing lining furnaces in the Ukraine, frankly.'

'Leave it with me,' said Brian. 'I'll have a word with Sir Dudley. He can probably clear it up.'

'Thanks.' Leo put down the phone. He finished going through the papers, and thought no more about it.

Sir Dudley had just finished a round of golf when Brian Bennett called him on his mobile.

'Sir Dudley, I've just been speaking to Leo Davies – he's been going through the documents that you passed to us recently.'

'Double Scotch for me, Alan,' said Sir Dudley to his friend, and went out to the lobby to take the call. The club didn't approve of members using their mobiles in the bar. 'What about them?'

'Well, it seems he's come across an invoice from a London company called Landline – ' Sir Dudley felt his heart tighten with alarm ' – to do with furnace linings. It's work which Zobil have apparently already invoiced for, so we were a bit puzzled. We wondered if you could help us.'

Sir Dudley told himself he was over-reacting. It was just an invoice, nothing to worry about. It was highly unlikely that the solicitors, or Leo Davies for that matter, would read anything suspicious into it. He racked his brains quickly for a plausible explanation to offer, but could think of none. He was careful to reply with as much nonchalance as he could muster.

'Sounds a little odd, certainly. I can't think how that's happened.' He paused. 'Is it of any particular importance, would you say?'

'No, probably not. We just wondered if you knew.'

'Afraid not. Now, Brian, if you don't mind, I'm rather busy –'

'Of course. Sorry to disturb you. I'm sure there's a simple explanation. We'll speak in the week.'

Sir Dudley said goodbye and clicked off his phone. He stood in the lobby, his mind racing. How could it have happened? What bloody fool had let that invoice slip through? He could only pray there weren't more suspicious documents among those papers. He reassured himself that the Landline invoice on its own wasn't incriminating – but if there were more like it, enough to form a paper trail, he hated to think where it might lead.

Alan, his golfing partner, strolled out from the bar. 'Your whisky's waiting for you.' He saw Sir Dudley's creased brow and anxious eyes. 'Some problem?'

Sir Dudley, who was still trying to work out what, if anything, he should do, glanced at his friend. 'What? Oh, just my solicitors getting their arses in a tangle over something – you know what these people are like. Insist on scrutinising every tiny detail. I'll be with you in a second. Just have to make a quick call.'

Alan went back into the bar. Sir Dudley picked up his train of thought. What he'd just said about scrutinising every tiny detail was about right – nothing escaped Leo Davies. It was what had impressed him about the man from the start. Utterly scrupulous, on top of every single aspect of the case. It was something they both had in common – that need to be in control, which Sir

Dudley understood only too well. Davies had been sufficiently concerned about the double invoice to ring Brian, and if no satisfactory explanation was immediately forthcoming, he wouldn't let the matter rest there. He'd want to find out the reason. And if he did...

Sir Dudley felt panic rising in his breast. It was a feeling he detested – he needed to get on top of this thing, to make sure it was sorted out swiftly, so that the feeling would go away. Otherwise he knew what would happen – he'd start waking up every night after an hour's sleep, sweating, brain going overtime. He'd been there before. He had to contain this.

He went outside and walked towards the first green, well away from the clubhouse. He couldn't take a chance on this phone call being overheard by anyone. Swiftly he tapped in Viktor's phone number. Come on, you bugger, answer, he thought, as the number at the other end rang and rang. He didn't want to have to leave a message. He needed to speak to Viktor now, urgently. He tried to fight down the sensation of panic swelling beneath his ribs. At last Viktor answered.

'Viktor? It's Dudley. Look, my solicitor's just been on to me. A Landline invoice has turned up in the papers they've got. .... Don't ask me how! Some dozy bloody fool at your end must have let it slip through! .... All right – but it's the only explanation I can think of. The point is, they're asking questions. They want to know why two invoices exist for the same work. .... No, Viktor, trust me – I have every reason in the world to worry. My barrister, Leo Davies, found this invoice, and he's not the kind of man to shrug his shoulders and forget about it. I know him. He's good, he's very clever – that's why I hired him in the first place. What? No, he's not suspicious *now*, necessarily, but when he starts digging around and trying to work out who Landline are and how they're involved – that's when he's going to get suspicious. .... No. Viktor, I can't pay him off. Why? Because he's not that kind of man! What do you mean, lawyers are the easiest? He's an English barrister, for God's sake – they have integrity. .... It means you can't get at them, you can't bribe them. No, I'm

51

not even going to try. It would blow the whole thing. This is your people's mess, so it's up to you to sort it out ... No, I don't know how! Just do it!'

Sir Dudley switched off his phone. He never enjoyed an irate conversation with Viktor. From the very beginning of his dealings with him, he'd had to work at maintaining a position of dominance without getting on the wrong side of the man. At least he felt easier now that he'd spoken to him. Whatever else he was, Viktor was someone who could be trusted to take care of things. In his own way, of course. Sir Dudley didn't think he'd have to worry about that Landline invoice. Viktor would probably find a way of stealing it, or destroying it, and then no one would be any the wiser.

Viktor Kroitor, an enterprising thirty-eight-year-old Ukrainian whose business interests included illegal arms trading, drug dealing, and the trafficking of prostitutes, and who had for the past year been laundering his profits through one of Sir Dudley Humble's London companies, switched off his mobile phone and slipped it into the inside pocket of his leather jacket. He disliked Sir Dudley when he panicked and started squealing like a pig. He disliked him anyway. Viktor turned his attention back to the pretty girl, Irina, who sat opposite him in the coffee shop in Odessa.

He nodded intently at her, focusing his attention away from Sir Dudley's problems. 'Yes, like I say – it's a good club, a really nice club. They always need dancers for the cabaret.' He swung a neat finger at her, pointing it like a gun, and smiled his attractive smile. He had dark, slicked-back hair, a heavy face with big, friendly eyes, and designer-stubble beard and moustache. 'I've seen you in the gym. You're a nice mover. Have you had dance lessons? No? You move like you have.'

The girl smiled, flattered. A job in the West would be fantastic – if she could just find work for two years or so, she could earn enough to come back and carry on her studies. At the moment she didn't have enough to buy books or pay her fees.

All she needed was the right opportunity – and Viktor Kroitor seemed to be offering it. Irina had heard stories of girls getting into bad trouble when they tried to move to the West, but Viktor Kroitor knew her brother, and her brother said he was a good guy. Looking at his face, and his smiling eyes, she felt that too. She trusted Viktor Kroitor.

'How much would it cost? I haven't got a lot of money.'

Viktor shrugged. 'I don't mind helping you with the air fare. I could even help you pay for dance lessons when you get there.' He shucked a cigarette from a packet and lit it. 'Don't worry. You can pay me back when you're earning enough. It's not a problem. I like helping people.' He offered her a cigarette and she took one. Viktor lit it for her. He sat staring at her, his dark eyes apparently studying her face. In fact, Viktor was thinking about Sir Dudley's problem, and trying to decide whether he should send one of his men to deal with it or attend to it himself. He smoked and considered. The girl Irina wondered why he was gazing at her so intently. It was nice, but not nice. Perhaps she should make conversation, but she couldn't think of anything to say. No, thought Viktor, best to handle it himself. Besides, there was this girl here. She was so beautiful, and very possibly a virgin – it would be a real pleasure to make sure she got properly settled into her new job in the west, and to do it personally. He stubbed out his cigarette and spoke. 'That phone call just now – I may have to go to London on business very soon. We can travel together, if you like.'

'Yes, I'd like that.' Irina nodded. The idea of going to another country was scary enough, but if she had a companion, someone who knew what he was doing, and whom she trusted, it would be much better. Viktor was a businessman – he dressed well, he had money and knew people. She would feel more confident in a strange country if he was there to introduce her. 'I've got a part-time job, but I don't think finishing will be a problem.'

'Fine.' Viktor nodded in a businesslike way. 'I'll need your passport so that I can fix the flight. Bring it with you tomorrow and I'll arrange everything.'

'And the job at the club?'

Viktor smiled. 'I'll talk to my friend this evening.'

When the girl had gone, Viktor sat and thought about what Dudley had told him. A nuisance, yeah, but one that was easily dealt with. He had never in his life heard of a lawyer who couldn't be bribed, but if Sir Dudley thought that was a bad idea – fine. There were plenty of other ways of persuasion. Or dissuasion. He took out his mobile phone and tapped in the number of a contact in London.

'Miron? Hi, this is Viktor. I need some information on a man. His name is Leo Davies.' A pause. 'That's about all I know. He is a barrister, a lawyer of some kind. I need you to find out all you can about him – where he lives, where he goes, what he does, family, friends. You know the kind of thing.' Viktor laughed. 'That's right. He's someone we need to bring into line.'

11

The weekend was so glorious that Leo decided to drive down with Oliver to his country house near Oxford. The heat of the previous week had given way to softer, moister weather, slaking the dry fields and turning the woods dense and lush again. The Oxfordshire house, set back from the road in a large garden fringed with trees, was very different from the smart house in Chelsea, with its white-walled rooms and clean, minimalist furnishings. Here an atmosphere of haphazard, cosy charm prevailed. The dark, polished floorboards were scattered with rugs, and the armchairs and sofas were high-backed and piled with cushions. There was an air of restfulness and comfort which was missing from the Chelsea house, as though both places represented two irreconcilable facets of Leo's own personality.

A log basket filled with toys and old books stood by the fireplace in the living room, and while Oliver emptied the contents of this on to the floor, Leo rang some old friends who lived in the neighbourhood and invited them to supper that evening. Then, after a brisk lunch of scrambled eggs on toast, he and Oliver went out to comb the lanes of Oxfordshire for black-berries. Before they left, Leo cut a few apples and potatoes into chunks, so that Oliver could feed the horses in the farmer's field at the end of the lane. He hoisted Oliver up so that he could perch on the gate, and the horses came ambling over the grass with friendly curiosity. As he held him, Leo could feel his son's small body tensing with excited pleasure. He handed Oliver some pieces of apple and potato, and Oliver held them out, giggling and shivering at the soft, whiskery touch of the horses' lips as they snaffled the food from his outstretched palm. The feeling of his son's small, robust body beneath his grasp filled

Leo with a deep sense of pleasure. When the food was all gone he kissed the top of Oliver's dark, glossy head and lifted him down.

They spent a couple of hours wading around the bramble bushes at the edge of the woods, picking fruit, while Oliver chattered to his father about all the preoccupations of his four-year-old life, including his new school. Leo detected, beneath Oliver's excited prattle about his new blazer and school bag, a trace of apprehension, so he told Oliver about his own first day at school, and how quickly you got used to things and made new friends. For a moment Leo found himself recalling, as if it were yesterday, the tarmac playground of the village school, surrounded by black railings that had seemed so high once, filled with roistering children. Himself and thirty eight mixed infants in one class, most of them wearing hand-me-downs, with one pair of shoes to do a year, and a box of coloured pencils that you daren't lose, because your mam couldn't afford another one. How different it would be for Oliver, in his fine new uniform, at his expensive school where the children were doubtless twelve to a class at most – children who would expect, and receive, yearly ski trips and outrageously expensive birthday parties and the latest electronic toys and computer games. Would he have wanted anything different for Oliver? Probably not, but he wished Rachel had given him a say. As it was, Kingswood House, with its privileged pupils from well-off, middle class, West London families was a *fait accompli*.

He glanced down at Oliver. His fingers and mouth were purple with berry juice, he had bramble stains on his sweat shirt and trousers, and a handful of rather mushy berries in his bag.

Oliver, aware of his father's gaze, looked up at him and saw the full bag of blackberries which Leo had picked.

'Daddy, you've got loads more than me!' He held up his own pathetic pickings.

'That's because I didn't eat most of mine.' Leo took the plastic bag from Oliver's damp grasp. 'Here.' He tipped some of his own haul into Oliver's bag and they set off down the lane for home, Oliver bumping his bag of blackberries happily against his thigh, depositing yet more stains for Rachel to fuss over.

Back at the house, Leo gave Oliver a quick wipe-over and put the blackberries in a bowl in the fridge, then they got into the car and went shopping for food for the evening. Leo's plan was to give Oliver tea at around half six, then put him to bed shortly after Alasdair and Jenny arrived for dinner. After they'd got back and unloaded the shopping, Leo cooked pasta with tomato sauce for Oliver, and then Oliver helped Leo to make an apple and blackberry crumble with the fruit they had picked that afternoon. Oliver stood on a chair to stir the crumble mix and Leo helped him to tip it on to the apples and blackcurrant mixture in the dish, and put it in the oven.

'You can have some before you go to bed,' Leo told him, 'but first you need to have a bath and scrub all those berry stains off properly. Mummy wouldn't like you with purple fingers.'

'Mummy likes everything clean,' said Oliver. 'Clean as clean.'

How true, thought Leo. Hers was an antiseptic world. It was up to Leo to add a dash of friendly grubbiness to Oliver's starched little life.

By half seven Leo was sitting in an armchair with a glass of whisky, watching the evening news while Oliver, freshly bathed and in his pyjamas, played on the rug with his toys. Leo heard the crunch of car wheels on the gravel outside, and went to greet his guests. Alasdair was in his mid-fifties, and had given up life at the Bar to become a journalist, contributing articles and commentaries to one of the broadsheets. His wife, Jenny, who ten years ago had been solicitor at the firm where Rachel worked, now ran a small, local picture-framing business.

Jenny made a fuss of Oliver while Leo dispensed drinks. Alasdair stood sipping his drink and watching Jenny and Oliver playing with a plastic tipper-truck.

'He's a lovely boy,' said Alasdair, 'but I can't help feeling grateful that our two are off our hands. Ruinously expensive things, kids.'

'I just wish I had more time with Oliver,' said Leo. 'I only see him every other weekend.'

'I know the feeling – fifteen years ago, when I was working all the hours God sent, I hardly ever saw Toby and Ed. Now I get all my work done at home, rarely have to go up to London, thank God.'

'Don't you miss the Bar?'

'Now and then. Miss the conviviality. But if I had a young family, I'd jump ship straight away. Having said that – ' Alasdair sipped his beer ' – communications being what they are now, there's probably no need. Who needs to be in an office, when you've got the phone and the internet?'

'True.'

'I'm surprised you stay up in London, when you have this place. Couldn't you get a good deal of your work done here?'

'I suppose so,' said Leo, 'but I have to go to court. Besides, I like London.'

'So do I,' said Jenny, getting up a little stiffly from the floor. 'Whatever Al says, I need my bi-monthly fix of shopping and people. Thank God we have the little place in Pimlico.'

'Ah,' said Leo, 'so you haven't cut your ties altogether?' He put down his drink and began to clear away Oliver's toys.

'No,' admitted Alasdair, 'but I still think anyone who lives in that hell-hole on a permanent basis is stark-staring mad.'

'Or has a living to earn.'

'That's my point. Barristers are self-employed creatures. Historically they've banded together in sets of chambers through physical necessity and financial convenience. But with technology improving every year, in theory most of them are already able to work wherever they want – apart from court appearances, of course. I think the physical point of having sets of chambers will become redundant in time.'

'I think perhaps you're taking a somewhat utilitarian view of the Bar. There's more to it than work, you know.' Leo stooped to pick up Oliver. 'Come on, young man – time for bed.'

'You said I could have some pudding!' said Oliver clasping his hands around his father's neck and gazing at him with challenging blue eyes.

'So I did,' said Leo. 'Come and show Jenny and Al what a clever cook you are.'

When Oliver had had his crumble and some milk, and was tucked safely in bed, Leo cooked steaks and made a salad, and the three of them ate at the big wooden table in the kitchen. After a few glasses of wine Jenny, as usual, began to quiz Leo solicitously about his love life. She was convinced that it was just a question of finding Leo the right woman. Leo, to satisfy her curiosity, told them about Anthea.

Later, when they were leaving, Jenny said, 'Next time you come down, bring your girlfriend – we could do with a bit of glamour around here!'

Leo went back into the quiet house and began to clear up the dishes and coffee cups. Then he poured the remains of the wine into a glass and took it through to an armchair in the living room. Perhaps he should bring Anthea down some weekend. Maybe when he next had Oliver – Oliver was such a sucker for a pretty face. And Anthea, for all her frivolity, wasn't as shallow as she pretended. Leo had found himself growing rather fond of her. She was amusing, she was affectionate, her attitude towards her own appetites was robust and uncomplicated, yet for all the intimacy they shared, she kept a part of herself at a charming distance. Leo found that intriguing and attractive. He liked her friends better than he had thought he would, too. Those he had met at the handful of dinner parties they'd been to were interesting, sensible, people, of a variety of ages. Lola was his favourite. Since she was Anthea's closest friend he had met her a number of times, and while she certainly didn't fall into the sensible category, Leo was naturally attracted by her funny and feckless nature, and by the fact that she was utterly unashamed of the idle, acquisitive life she led. She had an irresistible charm, much like Anthea. So perhaps he and Anthea had the potential to take their relationship further than he had thought. He dreaded another entanglement of the intense emotionality he had experienced with Rachel, but maybe if he and Anthea could maintain the equilibrium they had created so far —

Then he stopped himself. No – he had travelled a little way down this road before, and it didn't lead anywhere he wanted to go. Lovers were enough. He didn't want anyone permanent in his life, except Oliver. He had all the permanence he needed in chambers – that place, and the people in it, were all he needed to keep him grounded. His mind began to drift to what Alasdair had said about the joys of working from home. Perhaps there was something in it. If he didn't have to go into chambers every day, he'd be able to take Oliver to school some mornings, perhaps even pick him up mid-afternoon. A bit of flexibility in his life would mean he could see much more of his son, instead of every other weekend.

Leo yawned, too tired to think any more. Tomorrow he and Oliver would go to a friend of Jenny and Alasdair's for a lunchtime barbecue, and Oliver would be able to play with other kids. Then in the evening they would pack up and trek back to London in time for Oliver's big first day at school.

12

Leo dropped Oliver off at Rachel's house early on Sunday evening, together with his new pencil case and a couple of books which Leo had given him.

'I'm afraid his clothes got a bit stained when we were out blackberrying,' said Leo, handing over Oliver's overnight bag and teddy bear.

Rachel didn't seem concerned. 'Don't worry about that. Have you time for a coffee? I need to ask you something.' Leo followed her through to the kitchen, while Oliver went upstairs to his room.

'I won't have any coffee, thanks,' said Leo, wary of any extended conversation with Rachel. 'I've got some work to catch up on at home. What was it you wanted to ask?'

'I wondered if you'd mind having Ollie next weekend as well. I know you don't usually have him two weekends in a row – ' She smoothed back her dark hair with pale, hesitant hands.

'Of course I don't mind. I'd love to. Why? Some emergency?'

Rachel looked faintly embarrassed. 'Not quite. You'll probably think it's pretty frivolous, but Kate has arranged a weekend at Champney's. Just the two of us – a girlie thing. I gather it's a surprise for my birthday.' Leo felt a flash of guilt. He had forgotten it was Rachel's birthday soon. 'I mean, just say if it's a problem – '

'I've already said it's fine. I'm sure you could do with some relaxation and pampering. You're looking look a bit fed up these days.'

Rachel looked down at her hands. 'I am, I suppose.' She paused and then smiled. 'It's sweet of her to arrange it, really.' There was another pause. 'So is it all right if I drop him off with you on Saturday morning?'

'Fine.'

'And I'll pick him up on Sunday evening.'

Leo nodded. 'You could have told me all this tomorrow. I'll be seeing you in the morning, remember? You and Oliver?'

Her expression was vague, slightly guarded. 'Oh – yes, of course.'

Leo turned and headed back towards the hallway. 'The little guy's very excited about starting school. I just hope he's going to enjoy it.'

'Of course he will – it's a lovely school.'

'I'm sure it is. By the way – ' He turned as he reached the door ' – I meant to ask you. What about the fees? Just let me know how much, and I'll let you have the money.'

'Leo – ' Rachel hesitated for a moment. ' – you were very generous when we split up. More than you had to be. And I earn a pretty good salary, you know. I can afford his school fees.'

'Well, let me make a contribution. He's my son, too, you know. It was bad enough that you went ahead and chose a school without involving me, so at least I'd like to feel his education isn't completely out of my hands.'

'That isn't fair. You know I do the best for him.'

'Exactly – *you*. It's all you. What say do I have? None.'

'You did your bit after the divorce, Leo. Leave it at that.'

'Leave it at that? Rachel, I need to feel I'm part of his life. I'm his father, for God's sake, not some kindly uncle. If I can't help to pay for his schooling, then I'm not really entitled to have any say, am I?'

There was a long pause. Rachel folded her arms and said quietly, 'That's right. That's what I want.'

Leo laughed in disbelief. 'Oh, I get it. I'm just someone who borrows him every other weekend. Apart from that, he's nothing to do with me.'

'More or less.' Rachel had been avoiding Leo's gaze. Now she looked directly at him; her expression was pinched and nervous, and had lost any trace of vulnerability. 'I don't really want you to have any say in what happens to him, Leo. He goes to you

62

every other weekend against my better judgement. He loves you, and I would never deny him contact with his father. But I do have the right to restrict the influence you have on him, so far as I can.'

'What are you talking about?'

'You know what I'm talking about. The life you lead.'

'Oh, please!'

'You went down to the Oxford house this weekend – how do I know who else was there? One of your lovers? Maybe more? Men? Women?'

'Oh, for Christ's sake! We went blackberrying! We fed the horses! I had friends to dinner – and no, we didn't go on to have a full-blown orgy in the living room! When will you get it into your head that I'm a responsible parent? That I love my son? That I want to contribute to his life and well-being in every way I can? And that I'd like to have a say in choosing his school and paying the fees, if you don't mind!'

'Well, it's too late. I've paid them. It's not important, anyway.'

'No, what's important are all the things – the inaccurate things – you've just implied about the way I live.'

'So sue me, Leo. You're such a great fucking lawyer – go on.'

Leo shook his head. He might as well have had the coffee – this was always coming. Or had he started it? He had no idea. He glanced to the top of the stairs, anxious that Oliver might hear their raised voices. He lowered his tone, trying to be calm and moderate. 'Enough. This is going nowhere. I shall be outside his school tomorrow at eight forty five. On the dot. And don't try to smuggle him in without letting me see him. I mean it.' He went to the foot of the stairs and called up. 'Oliver!'

There was a thump from above, then feet crossing the floor, and then Oliver appeared on the landing. 'Come and give me a hug before I go.' Oliver bounced downstairs and hugged his father. 'I'll see you in the morning, old fellow,' said Leo, and dropped a kiss on his head. Then he left, saying nothing more to Rachel.

As he drove back, he tried to bank down his anger. Was this a cumulative thing? Was she going to start poisoning Oliver's mind against him in a few years' time? He wouldn't put it past her. Her mother had been a bitch of the first order, as he recalled, so maybe Rachel was headed that way. No – not possible. No matter how badly their relationship might have ended, she was essentially a fair, decent person. So was there some justice in what she said about his influence on Oliver? Perhaps in the past, but not any more. It was just a question of making her see that, of eradicating these notions she had about the way he lived his life. Easier said than done.

13

In a cheap hotel room somewhere in Bayswater, Irina Karpacheva sat on the edge of a bed, picking listlessly at the worn candlewick bedspread. Through the thin wall she could hear the muted rumble of men's voices, together with the reedy sound of some other girl crying. She had done her own crying. She felt empty of tears, utterly drained. The fact of her own naive stupidity lay upon her like a dead weight. Just a week ago she had willingly, smilingly, handed her passport to Viktor Kroitor so that he could buy her plane ticket to England. She had sat next to him on the plane, everything had been fine and friendly. Then when they'd got to the hotel in London, things had changed. He'd asked her for the money for the plane ticket and the hotel, which of course she didn't have. Viktor had told her she'd have to pay off her debt, that he'd keep her passport until she did – and by work he didn't mean dancing in a cabaret. That job had never existed.

Since then she had been moved twice, but the shabby hotels were much alike, and she had no idea where she was. She knew nothing about London. The last place had been better because she'd been with other girls, and they could talk, in between men. The men. It had got to the point where Irina wished it might be Viktor, instead of these strangers, because at least she knew him. At least he had once seemed like a friend. But that first time with Viktor had taught her how wrong she was. He was a beast.

She got up and went to the window, pushed one of the short, plush purple curtains aside and tried to look down, to see what was below and where it led to. But the room was high up, and the building next door was so close that her vantage point was poor; all she could see was a black metal fire escape leading down from the other building. What was the point of thinking about getting away? She was watched constantly. Viktor had her passport. He'd told her that everything about her situation was illegal, and that if she tried to leave, she'd be arrested and put in jail. Then she'd never get home.

There was a light knock on the door. Irina moved away from the window, eyes fixed apprehensively on the door as it opened. It was Marko, the big guy who was employed by Viktor to fetch cigarettes, guard the girls, and perform any menial criminal tasks which might crop up. Irina didn't know whether to be relieved or frightened. So far Marko had been decent to her, in a gruff way. But why was he here, in her room? Had Viktor and his gangster friends decided to offer her for free as a reward for some service or other?

Marko closed the door and stood there for a moment. 'Hi,' he said.

'Hi,' replied Irina cautiously. 'What do you want?'

He shrugged his beefy shoulders. He seemed a little awkward. 'I'm off my shift. I wondered if you'd like a game of cards.' He paused. 'In case you're bored.' He shrugged again. 'I'm bored.'

It was a pleasure to Irina to hear someone speaking in Ukrainian – not brutally, or peremptorily, but in a casual, off-hand way. Such a small thing to make her heart glad. Still, she was suspicious. It was impossible to trust anyone who had anything to do with Viktor. 'I haven't got any playing cards,' she replied.

'It's OK – I have some,' said Marko. He fumbled inside his jacket pocket with a bearlike candour which somehow reassuring, and produced a battered pack of cards.

Irina nodded. Anything to relieve the tedium. And if he tried to push his luck – well, she'd worry about that when it happened. 'Yeah, fine,' she said, and sat down on the bed. Marko pulled a chair over from the dressing table, sat down, took the cards from the pack, and began to shuffle them.

14

The week started well. Oliver settled in happily on his first day at school, and Leo went off to the Temple in an upbeat mood – but thereafter things went pretty rapidly downhill. He had to chair three committee meetings – finance, management and recruitment – and all of them seemed remarkably ill-tempered. What, Leo wondered, was the reason for the current general air of dissatisfaction? Was he to blame, as head of chambers? He didn't recall all this disharmony when Roderick had been head, or Cameron Renshaw. Perhaps his 'people management skills', as Maurice like to call them, were to blame. As for Maurice – things were not good with Maurice. He was now quite unapologetically two months' behind on his rent, on top of which one of the pupils had come to Leo to complain that Maurice had groped her – well, not quite, but near enough – and the last thing they needed in chambers was a sexual harassment suit. Maurice had continued to make low-level mutterings about bringing contempt proceedings against Leo in relation to the anti-suit injunction, and then on Wednesday Roger and Maurice had had a stand-up row on the staircase, which ended in doors being slammed and a hush of embarrassment descending on the building. That kind of thing didn't help.

By Friday, Leo was feeling somewhat depressed.

'What the hell am I doing wrong?' he asked Anthony.

'It's not you. It's the rumblings of revolution. I think you'll find out pretty soon. I gather Roger is planning to talk to you.'

And indeed, an hour later Roger put his head round Leo's door and invited him to go for a drink that evening. 'Marcus is coming, and Alison and Simon.'

A delegation, thought Leo, and felt apprehensive.

Since the weekend the weather had gone from mild and showery to grey and thundery, and the four of them sat in a corner of the pub while the rain outside splashed on the flagstones of Devereux Court. Simon bought drinks for all, and after a few moments of uneasy chat, Roger took the initiative.

'We have a proposition for you,' he told Leo.

'Oh?' Leo looked from face to face. He had assumed they'd brought him here to make some kind of private complaint. 'What kind of proposition?'

'A business one.' There was a long pause, then Roger said, 'We're thinking of setting up another set of chambers.'

Leo digested this information. Was he surprised? Perhaps he should have seen it coming. He took a sip of his beer and said, 'I see.'

'A set of virtual chambers,' continued Roger.

Leo frowned. 'I don't follow. What do you mean – virtual?'

'In the sense that it wouldn't really exist. Only it would. That is to say, the nexus would exist, but not the physical reality.'

'Roger, I know you've always been a big fan of *The Matrix*, and perhaps you see yourself as the Keanu Reeves of the Middle Temple, but – '

'A limited company,' interrupted Marcus, a handsome, black barrister who had been listening impassively till this moment. 'Instead of the traditional set-up, where all chambers liabilities are those of the head of chambers, who is indemnified, the idea would be to take the functions of chambers and devolve them to a company – a service company, if you like. It would take a regular payment from each tenant, rather in the way we presently pay chambers' rent, in return for which the company would be responsible for all the administrative decisions.'

'I still don't understand the 'virtual' part.'

'There would be no chambers. No building. No rooms. Everyone would work from home.'

'But how would you bring in work? Who's going to do that?'

'We'd still have clerks. They'd be the people running the company. Peter Weir reckons we'd need two – '

'Peter Weir?' exclaimed Leo, somewhat surprised. Peter was a clerk in his early thirties who had joined 5 Caper Court a couple of years ago. Smart and capable, he was a member of a new breed of clerk, who had none of the old below-stairs ethos – they saw themselves not so much as clerks as facilitators, business managers.

'A lot of this was his idea,' said Roger. 'Two clerks responsible for marketing chambers, for billing, credit control, returning briefs, and general admin, and someone to handle incoming briefs.'

'Well, stop right there. What about briefs? How would they be distributed?'

'DX – documents exchange,' said Alison. 'Either that or email. People just pick up instructions from a postbox, or on their computers.'

For once in his life, Leo was struggling to grasp something. 'But you couldn't – I mean – ' He fought for words, trying to imagine the unimaginable – the sweeping away of chambers, the very fabric of every barrister's existence, the physicality on which they depended. 'What about conferences, meetings?'

'Easy enough to rent a place for the purpose of conferences and arbitrations. You don't need a whole building.'

'And court? You lot spend half your time in court.'

'Not that much,' replied Alison. 'Some of it, admittedly. But I haven't been in court at all this week. More and more hearings in judges' chambers take place by phone, and it's only a matter of time before we have video conferencing.'

'Have you ever conducted a contested application at an inter-locutory stage by phone?' asked Leo. 'It's an appalling business. You lose everything that's valuable about face-to-face advocacy – body language, inflections, expression. I don't see that as a tremendous advance.'

'It does allow you to stick two fingers up at the other side if you feel like it,' said Simon with a grin.

'The fact is,' went on Marcus, 'all of us could work perfectly well at home and simply come up to town when we have a court hearing. There's no need to spend all day in a building full of people working for themselves and getting together only to make decisions about rent and coffee machines.'

'Think about it – if you wanted to run a business efficiently, the last people you'd ask to do it would be a bunch of barristers,' said Roger. 'All this 'one man, one vote' business produces complete stasis, as often as not. Just think – no more problems with rent, or with people not paying on time. Prompt payment of fees. More money all round – the amount each tenant would pay the service company would be a lot less than the amount we currently pay in rent, obviously. And there would be the joy of not having to struggle in with the rest of the commuting world to the Temple every day.'

'Exactly,' agreed Simon. 'My life's a logistical nightmare since we had the new baby. I have to drop my son off at school and then struggle in to work. I hate it.'

'It's the same for me,' said Alison. 'I'm paying about two thirds of my earnings to employ a full-time nanny. If I worked from home, I could come to a much more flexible, cheaper arrangement, and I'd see more of my daughter. I'd rather adjust my work to fit my life.'

'Which is exactly what a virtual chambers is all about – you work where you like, when you like. In short, individually we run our own show, and the collective business is taken care of by the company.'

All four of them sat over their drinks, gazing at Leo like schoolkids who had just produced to a teacher incontrovertible arguments in support of an outlandish proposition.

There was silence for a moment. Then Leo asked, 'What about pupils? How do you train the next generation of barristers outside the context of chambers?'

'Admittedly that's not easy. But it's not beyond the realms of possibility to have someone working with you at home.'

'Hardly ideal. And it points up the big flaw in your idea – in exchange for all the convenience and administrative efficiency and cost-saving, you lose everything that's valuable about people working in a shared environment. There's loss of tradition, conviviality – the collegiate spirit, as dear old Cameron used to call it.' Leo turned to Simon. 'Remember last night when you came to my room to ask me about that limitation of liability point? How are you going to do that in your virtual chambers?'

'I could always ring you up.'

'Yes, but you'd only ring me because you know me, and you only know me because we work alongside one another in the same set of chambers. That pool of knowledge is invaluable – and leaving aside the question of exchanging ideas and advice, there's the social aspect to consider. Putting your head round someone's door to have a chat, or invite them for a drink, for instance – the way you did this afternoon, Roger. And afternoon tea, the chambers' Christmas party. These things are not insignificant. They oil the wheels of life.'

'We'd still have the Christmas party,' said Alison. 'We could all get together in whatever place we use for cons, and stuff.'

'Wonderful. What a joy that would be.'

'Anyway,' said Roger, interrupting the silence that had fallen, 'that's our plan, and we wondered if you'd be interested.'

'Me?'

'Well, yes.' Roger seemed mildly embarrassed. 'One thing we would lose by leaving 5 Caper Court is prestige. We rather hoped we might make that up by having someone like you join us. Your name carries a lot of weight.'

'So you gain from my presence?' Leo was bemused. 'And what do I stand to gain?'

'Money. Flexibility. Same as the rest of us. And you wouldn't have the burden of responsibility you have now. Look, it's just an idea we're floating at present. Apart from you, we've only mentioned it to Anthony Cross and Juliet Gummer. We don't need an answer straight away. Just give it your consideration – there might be certain benefits that don't occur to you immediately.'

'It sounds as though your plans are pretty far advanced,' said Leo. He finished his beer. 'My inclination is to tell you you're all mad – but I'll do as you ask and think about it.'

'Good,' said Marcus. 'More drinks, everyone?'

'Not for me,' said Leo. 'I have to go. I'll leave you lot to it. Thanks for the drink. Night.'

He put on his raincoat and left. As he walked down the steps to Fountain Court, heading for his car, he tried to identify the feeling of melancholy which the discussion had induced in him. I'm getting old, he thought. To people like Roger, Marcus, Simon and Alison, all under thirty five, it was self-evident that progress dwelt in ever-advancing communications, in the flexibility they gave to life, the scope for living without reliance on others. But what about the importance of familiarity, of shared experience and surroundings, the comfort of being part of something constant, and yet permanently changing? He turned his collar up against the rain as he passed Middle Temple Hall, and glanced up at its dark, high portals. Not for the first time, it struck Leo that the Temple, his place of work for over twenty five years, represented more of a home to him than any place he had ever known. And such a home. Its emblem alone dated back to the 13th century, to the Knights Templar. Chaucer had depicted one of his characters as Middle Temple cook. One of the chief aims of Wat Tyler and his followers during the Peasant's Revolt had been to sack the Temple and throw out all the lawyers – not so far removed from the aims of Roger and his merry band, reflected Leo. How could they contemplate leaving a place of such history, such sentimental magnificence, merely to earn a few extra thousand and get up a little later in the mornings?

On the other hand, he had to admit there could be certain attractions in working from home. As he unlocked his car and got in, Leo recalled his conversation with Alasdair the previous weekend. Hadn't Al said that if he had his time over again he'd do it differently, shaping his work round his life, instead of the other way round? Leo drove along Embankment through the evening traffic, thinking it all through. One could see the advantages, certainly. No getting into chambers early to beat the rush hour, which seemed to get worse with each passing month.

None of the hassle of being head of chambers – a job where the burdensome responsibilities far outweighed any notional prestige. No need to worry about billing figures, about Maurice, or having to chair endless committees. He'd even be able to collect Oliver from school – in fact, come to think of it, work commitments permitting, he might be able to do it just about every day. Rachel could hardly object, since the present arrangement involved a child-minder picking Oliver up and having him for a few hours till Rachel got back from work. Leo recalled the acrimonious conversation they'd had last Sunday night, Rachel's self-confessed desire to limit Leo's influence on Oliver. That would scupper her plans. He would become a proper part of Oliver's life, helping him with his homework, getting to know about his friends and teachers, instead of just being an every-other-weekend fixture. By the time he reached Chelsea, he'd decided that maybe Roger was right. Perhaps the idea of their new venture possessed attractions which hadn't been apparent at first glance.

Leo drove home, showered and changed, and went out to a birthday party being thrown by a friend in a restaurant in St James's. Anthea had been in Bermuda since Wednesday, and wouldn't be back until tomorrow, so he was glad of the diversion. Lately he had begun to find evenings spent on his own in the house long and tedious.

Just before midnight, as he was leaving the restaurant, his mobile rang. At the other end was a young woman whose voice he didn't recognise, but who seemed to be in a state of some agitation.

15

At the same moment that Leo was saying goodnight to his friends in the restaurant, Lucy and Georgia were huddled in the ladies loo at Kabaret's Prospect, a fashionable Soho club, debating the finer points of their strategy.

'So, how drunk are you supposed to be? Like, totally hammered? Or just a bit out of it?'

'Not completely wasted, obviously.' Lucy shot a glance at her reflection and pulled the Chloe top a little further off her shoulders. 'Not vomiting in the gutter kind of thing. But pretty bad. Bad enough to ring someone up. Why not say you think someone might've spiked my drink?'

Georgia looked doubtful. 'Because he might want to call an ambulance. Or the police, or something.'

Lucy considered this. 'OK – but I've got to be more than just a bit tipsy. On the *way* to being wasted, maybe.'

'I don't think this is going to work. Isn't he going to think it totally weird that I'm ringing him, when I don't even know him?'

'Trust me – it will work. It's got to. Anyway, he's my sister's boyfriend. He'll feel he's got to look after me.'

'I didn't know he was your sister's boyfriend! That's like – immoral!'

'Yeah, well...' Lucy smudged a little more eyeliner on her lower lids. She met Georgia's gaze in the mirror and grinned. Georgia grinned back.

'My God, Lucy, you're so bad!'

'I can't help it.' She took her mobile phone from her bag, scrolled to Leo's number, and handed it to Georgia. 'Come on, let's do it.'

Leo had been on the brink of hailing a cab when his mobile rang. It had just begun to rain. He stepped back on to the pavement as he answered his phone, trying to make sense of the strange young woman at the other end.

'I'm sorry – do I know you? .... Georgia? A friend of Lucy's? Lucy who? No, I don't – ' The name registered. 'Anthea's sister? Well, I don't understand – why are you ringing me?' Leo scanned the street for more taxis as he listened; now that it had started to rain, he'd probably never get one. 'I see. Look, I don't want to be unhelpful, but I'm not sure what you expect me to do about it. I suggest you put her in a taxi and take her home .... She's gone where? .... When will she be back? I see. Then take her to her sister's flat. She has a key, as I understand it .... What – *all* of them?' Leo was feeling distinctly exasperated. 'Look, I really don't think I can help you. I barely know Lucy, and I'm sure you or some of her other friends are better able to – What? Well, why not?' Leo listened for another few seconds, then gave a sigh. 'Where are you? Right. I'll come in a taxi. Look after her till I get there.'

Georgia snapped the phone shut and she and Lucy doubled up, giggling.

'Ohmigod, he's really coming!' squeaked Lucy, when she'd got her breath back. 'Georgie, you were amazing! You sounded so, *so* worried! It was *so* convincing! And when you said that stuff about me losing my keys – '

'I know! I don't know how he ever believed that!'

'Cos you're a brilliant actress. My God, you deserve an Oscar.'

'He sounded really pissed off, though, Luce. Like he didn't want to know.'

'Of course he did. But he's coming, isn't he? Just leave the rest to me.'

'Well, start acting like you're smashed, because he'll be here soon. Come on, we'd better go upstairs and do our stuff on the pavement.'

Leo caught a cab and headed towards Soho, tired and extremely irate. He'd had quite a lot to drink at the restaurant, and the last thing he needed, at midnight on a Friday, was to have to rescue Anthea's drunk, twenty-something sister from the gutters of Soho. How had she got hold of his number? Anthea, he presumed. Well, if the girl was capable of instructing this Georgia friend of hers to ring it, then perhaps she wasn't in too bad a state. He hoped not. But if she was, better that he should bail her out than that the police should pick her up. Anthea wouldn't like that.

When he got to Dean Street the late night crowds were filling the streets, most of them drunk and raucous, and the atmosphere lent authenticity to the little vignette which Georgia and Lucy were putting together on the pavement outside the club. Lucy was leaning against the wall, apparently much the worse for wear, with Georgia steadying her and looking anxious. Leo's cab drew up on the corner, and Lucy clocked it through half-closed eyes.

'That's him,' she murmured to Georgia, her heart giving a little lurch at the gorgeous sight of him as he got out and told the cabbie to wait.

'Here he comes,' whispered Georgia. 'He looks annoyed.'

Lucy gave a little whimpering groan and slumped back against the wall. Leo, drawing closer, recognised Lucy and stopped. He glanced at Georgia. 'Hi – I'm Leo.' He gazed for a few seconds at Lucy. 'Right – she doesn't look too good. Isn't there anyone else with you?' He put out a hand to steady Lucy as she slid slightly sideways on the wall.

'No,' said Georgia. 'I don't know what to do with her.' My God, thought Georgia, he really was old – forty at least. Good looking, yeah, but totally ancient. She hoped Luce knew what she was doing.

A group of yelling youths swayed past; they leered and whistled at Lucy, who appeared to be almost comatose. This wasn't a healthy place for a vulnerable young woman late on a Friday night.

'Well, look – I suggest you take her back to your place,' said Leo wondering why this hadn't occurred to him earlier. 'Where do you live? You can take my cab, and I'll find another.'

This was unexpected. Thinking on her feet, Georgia said, 'I can't. I really can't. My mother would absolutely go ballistic if she saw Lucy like this. Lucy's mum's a friend of hers. Please – that's the last thing Lucy needs.'

It seemed a slightly odd thing for a twenty-something-year-old to say, but Leo supposed that if you lived with your parents, it was understandable. He even felt a little sorry for Lucy. Evidently her mother wasn't too concerned what her daughter got up to, since she seemed to be away a good deal. Someone had to look after her, and in the absence of Anthea, Leo supposed it was up to him.

He sighed. 'All right. She'd better come with me. Her sister will be back tomorrow, in any event.'

'Oh, thanks,' said Georgia, the relief in her voice not entirely feigned. She helped Leo to steer a stumbling Lucy to the cab waiting on the corner.

The cabbie looked over his shoulder at Lucy, who lay back against the seat with her eyes shut. 'I hope she's not going to start chucking up in the back of my cab.'

'I doubt it,' said Leo. 'Let's hope not, anyway.' He turned to Georgia. 'What about you? I can't just leave you here.'

'Um – I can get the bus,' said Georgia, who had other friends in the club whom she intended to rejoin any minute. 'Really – don't worry. I'll be fine. You look after Lucy. I'm so grateful.'

Georgia stood on the pavement and watched as the cab drove off. My God, you had to admit that Lucy had some nerve, doing what she was doing. Georgia couldn't wait to hear about it at school on Monday.

16

As the cab made its way towards Hyde Park, Lucy turned her head a little and glanced surreptitiously at Leo through half-closed eyes. He was gazing out at the traffic, his face grim. She gave a moan and a faint cough, and Leo turned to look at her. She opened fluttering eyelids.

'Lucy? How are you feeling?'

Aware that, for the sake of plausibility, her recovery mustn't appear too rapid, Lucy closed her eyes again, then after a few seconds muttered, 'Not too good.'

'I'm hardly surprised. How much did you have to drink?'

She put her hand to her head. 'I don't know. Not a lot.' Her eyes still closed, she put out a feeble hand and clutched his arm; it was magical just to be touching him.

'What's wrong? Are you going to be sick?'

She shook her head slowly, and decided to relapse into groggy silence for the remainder of the journey, with her hand resting on his sleeve. He didn't appear to mind.

By the time they reached Chelsea, Lucy reckoned it was OK for her to seem like she was a bit better. When Leo tried to help her out of the cab she said faintly, 'It's fine, I can manage.' When they got into the house – which Lucy, on a swift appraisal, thought was pretty cool – she decided for dramatic effect to go downhill for a minute or two. She fell into an armchair with a moan and closed her eyes. Leo dropped his jacket on the sofa and looked down at her.

'I'll make us both some coffee.' He felt he could do with some – the birthday celebrations had been extremely good, but those last two brandies might have been a mistake. Then again, he hadn't anticipated having to rescue Anthea's ditzy little sister at the end of the evening.

While Leo was busy in the kitchen, Lucy sat up slowly and had a good look round. The room was furnished in expensive good taste, with leather sofas and armchairs dotted around the spotless, blonde wood floor, discreetly-placed lighting accentuating carefully positioned pictures and pieces of sculpture. Two uplighters cast an intimate glow around the room. Lucy slipped off her red shoes and raked her fingers through her hair, waiting for Leo to return.

He brought through a tray with a cafetière and two cups, and set it down on a glass-topped table near to Lucy's chair.

'Thanks,' said Lucy weakly, as he handed her a cup. 'I'm feeling a bit better now.'

Leo regarded her as she sipped her coffee. 'You seem to have made a rapid recovery,' he observed. 'You can't have been very drunk.'

'I wasn't,' said Lucy. 'I just began to feel really awful when I was in the club. Sort of faint and dizzy. I can't think what it was.' She gave him a doleful little smile. 'Thank you so much for coming to get me.'

'That's all right. How did you manage to lose all your keys?'

'I don't know. I'm a bit dopey like that. Always losing things.' She lay back in the chair. Best not to appear too perky – the mood had to remain low-key. She glanced around slowly. 'This is a lovely room.'

'Thank you.' Leo sipped his coffee. He couldn't help noticing that the manner in which she lay sprawled in the large armchair was both provocative, but apparently entirely unselfconscious. Her little black satin skirt, which was diminutive enough in the first place, had ridden up, and he could glimpse the tops of her sheer black hold-up stockings, and the flimsy, but very pretty top she was wearing had slipped off one creamy shoulder. Her eyes, dark and distant as she glanced around the room, were large and childlike. To ward off the thoughts which had come unbidden to his mind, he rose and said, 'I'll go and check the bed's made up in the spare room.'

'Please stay and talk for a bit,' said Lucy, her voice still faint.

Leo hesitated. 'Did you enjoy the Kandinski exhibition?' she asked. She sounded like she wanted to talk to make herself feel better. He could understand that. He sat back down on the sofa.

They talked about the exhibition for ten minutes or so. A short silence fell, at the end of which Leo said, 'There's nothing really wrong with you, is there?'

Lucy gazed at him, then slowly shook her head. 'Not now. Not now I'm here. With you.' And to his astonishment she came in one gliding movement from her chair to where he sat, and knelt before him, her hands resting on his thighs. 'Leo, I just want to be with you.' Before he could say anything more, she rose up, put an arm around his neck, drew his face towards hers and kissed him. Her kiss was so deliciously tentative that for a few helpless seconds he found himself responding. He fought back the urge to kiss her more deeply and drew away.

'Did you do this on purpose?' asked Leo. She nodded, her eyes dark and huge. 'Jesus Christ,' he murmured, his voice a mixture of disbelief and regretful desire. He took her arm gently from around his neck. 'Lucy, I'm seeing your sister. Whatever you came here for is not going to happen.'

'Oh, yes it is,' she breathed. 'I want you so much, Leo. I've wanted you for ages. We're here now, just you and me, so we might as well enjoy it.' And she tried to press her mouth against his again. Leo grasped her upper arms and pushed her gently away.

'You set up that entire little charade just for this?'

'Don't sound like that. It'll be worth it, honestly.'

He stared at her curiously and intently for a moment, then said, 'Lucy – how old are you?'

She give a small, trembling smile. His touch seemed to have set her whole body on fire. She wanted very badly to kiss him again, to let her body melt into his, and let whatever he wanted to happen, happen. 'Seventeen,' she murmured.

'Seventeen? You're seventeen and you go around pulling stunts like this deliberately to seduce your sister's – ' He groped for a word ' – men-friends?'

'Oh, Leo, it'll be lovely. I want you to teach me – everything.' Her lips were perilously close to his; her breath smelt like clover, and her skin beneath his fingers was soft and young. She was every dirty old man's dream, thought Leo, which made him ... But the very next thing she said appalled him. 'I've never made love to anyone before. I want you to be the first. Please.' She had begun to unfasten the little crystal buttons of her blouse.

Leo let out a short laugh, though he felt like crying. 'Stop,' he said; but she didn't seem to hear him, and tried to kiss him again. 'Lucy – ' He grasped her shoulders as her flimsy top fell open, and shook her – not hard, but hard enough to make her look at him properly, clearly, like someone waking up. 'Lucy, I have no intention of doing anything with you, or to you. Do you under-stand? This is the worst idea you have ever had in your young life, believe me. Leaving aside your age, and what you've just told me, it's not my habit to sleep with the sisters of my girlfriends.' As he said this, Leo tried to recall whether it was strictly accurate or not. Probably not.

She looked at him in astonishment. 'Don't you want me? Why don't you want me?' Tears filled her lovely eyes. 'Leo, I love you so much!'

Firmly but gently, and feeling older than he ever had done, Leo said, 'No, you don't, I promise you. This is all a huge, rather silly mistake.' She gazed at him miserably with damp eyes, her mouth wobbling a bit, tendrils of dark hair around her young face, blouse hanging open to expose small, rosy breasts. She was temptation incarnate, thought Leo. He lifted his hands from her shoulders and began to do up her buttons one by one. Then taking her gently by the hands, he stood up, bringing her to her feet, and said, 'You'll have to stay here tonight, because frankly I don't know what else to do with you. But I don't want to hear one more word of this nonsense about me and you. Not a word. Do you understand?'

He meant it, Lucy realised. Oh God, he meant it. She'd thought it was going to be so easy, so perfect. And he sounded just like – just like one of her teachers, the way he was speaking to her. Why did everyone have to treat her like a child? Why didn't he believe her when she said she loved him? She hated him for not believing her, and for not wanting her. She couldn't believe he didn't. She *so* couldn't believe it!

Lucy burst into tears. Leo regarded her sadly. Nothing would have given him greater pleasure, truly, than to remove every inadequate piece of clothing from her glorious young body and have her right here on the sofa. But there were limits, even for him. When she had quietened down a bit, he said, 'Come on. I'll show you where you can wash your face. Then you need to get to bed. You're a bit overwrought. You'll feel better in the morning.'

Sniffling, Lucy picked up her shoes and allowed herself to be escorted upstairs. Leo showed her into a bedroom with a connecting bathroom, said goodnight, and left her alone.

He went downstairs and cleared up the coffee cups, then locked up. He stood for a moment in the middle of the room, where the faintest trace of her teenage perfume still hung in the air. He drew his hands wearily across his face, then switched the lights off and went to bed, locking the door of his room – whether for her protection or his, he wasn't sure.

17

Only at three in the morning, when the after-effects of the brandy had jerked him into heart-racing wakefulness, did it occur to Leo that Lucy, of course, hadn't lost her keys, and that he could have taken her home after all. Too late. He lay there in the darkness, wondering quite how this whole episode would play with Anthea when he saw her next. Unable to get back to sleep, he got up and went downstairs for a glass of water. Then he went back to bed, forgetting to lock his door. Four hours later, as early light pearled the room, he woke again to find Lucy, entirely naked, slipping beneath the duvet.

She laid her head on the neighbouring pillow and gazed at him. Her eye make-up from the night before had left panda smudges beneath her eyes, but apart from that, she looked fresh as a daisy, and ridiculously adorable. Leo, on the other hand, felt old and groggy and unshaven, and already very tired of this game.

He yawned, then said wearily, 'Lucy, I meant what I said last night.' She said nothing. 'Anyway, this early morning encounter is probably a good thing. It should put you off me for life. Now, go on – get out of my bed and get dressed. I'm taking you home.'

'Leo, why don't you want me?' She put out a hand to his face, and Leo was swept with a wave of hungover irritation. He sat up and gripped her fingers before they could touch him; all he wanted was this tiresome, clinging girl out of his bed and his life. The situation was enough to make him momentarily lose his temper. 'Why?' he snapped. 'Because you're a destructive, tedious child who has no idea what she's doing, and who likes playing stupid games without any thought of the consequences for other people! And I want rid of you!'

Lucy's eyes darkened. 'You're a bastard. You know that? And you've got morning breath.'

'Good – a touch of real life at last.' Leo sighed and lay back on the pillow. 'Perhaps it'll make you realise how daft this all is. You silly kid – what on earth are you doing, going around offering yourself to middle-aged men? Haven't you got any self-respect?' The ache in his head was becoming worse.

'You're so horrible!' Lucy flounced from beneath the duvet like an angry nymph, and grabbed Leo's shirt from the chair where he had thrown it last night. She put it on. 'I don't know why I went to all this trouble!'

'Nor do I. Now, you can repay my hospitality by going downstairs and making me some coffee. Go on.'

She left the room, banging the door and thumping downstairs. Children, thought Leo. He supposed he should be flattered, but he wasn't. The last thing he wanted was to be the object of some teenage fixation. After a few moments he got up, pulled on a pair of boxers, and went to the bathroom to find some paracetamol.

It was then that he heard the doorbell. It took him some seconds to think who it could be. Then he remembered – Rachel. She was going to Champneys, and bringing Oliver over. Recent events had put it completely out of his mind.

'Oh, my Christ,' muttered Leo, and hurried out to the landing to call to Lucy not to answer the door.

Too late. He reached the top of the stairs to see Lucy, fetchingly clad in one of his Valentino shirts with only two of the buttons done up, opening the front door to Rachel, who was standing on the doorstep holding Oliver's hand. They stared at Lucy, and then up at him.

It was a hellish moment. He was reminded forcibly of the time when Oliver was a baby, and Rachel had come back from a business trip abroad to find him in bed with the nanny. That had been bad, but at least then he'd been completely bang to rights. This time he was guilty of absolutely nothing whatsoever – even if he had been, there would be room for arguing that it was none of Rachel's business. However, in view of the fact that she was convinced he led a private life of squalor and depravity, and given the circumstantial evidence of a teenage girl answering his door in one of his shirts at eight thirty in the morning, things were not looking good.

To save his dignity, he went back to the bathroom, grabbed a towelling robe and put it on, and hurried downstairs. Lucy, having divined the potential of this situation for embarrassing Leo, was introducing herself to Rachel with a mixture of èlan and impudence.

'Get into the kitchen!' Leo told Lucy, his voice like thunder.

'No need,' said Rachel, stony-faced. 'We're going.' She turned and led Oliver back to the car. Leo followed, pulling the front door behind him.

'Rachel, hold on – this isn't what you think,' he said, marvelling at how sometimes only clichés would do. Rachel opened the rear door of the car and hustled Oliver in. Rachel closed the door, and Oliver's small face gazed at Leo through the window.

'Look,' said Leo, 'she's a friend's sister, a silly kid who got herself into a spot of bother in Soho last night. I had to go and rescue her – there wasn't anyone else to do it. She stayed the night at mine, and that's all. OK?'

'Leo,' said Rachel coldly, 'you think you're such a great lawyer that you can talk your way out of everything. Well, you're not in the Court of Appeal now. The fact is, you've been telling me lately that you've cleaned up your act, that I can rely on you to look after Oliver responsibly. And what happens? I bring him round, as planned, and some girl who looks no older than fourteen answers the door – someone you've evidently spent the night with. At least, I'm assuming she's the only one. Knowing you, there's probably half a dozen more in there, plus a couple of rent boys thrown in for good measure.' He tried to speak, but she carried on. 'And don't tell me it's none of my business, because what happens in a house where my son is to spend his weekend *is* my business!' She went round to the driver's side. 'I'll call Kate and tell her our trip is off.'

'There's no need,' said Leo, angry and exasperated. 'Everything I just told you is true, and the girl is leaving in ten minutes. It's perfectly fine for Oliver to stay. Why do you always have to jump to whatever conclusion suits your biased view of me?'

'Because it's invariably the right one!' She got into the car, slammed the door, and drove off.

Leo stood on the pavement for a moment, then, seeing a woman with a small dog on a lead approaching, went back to the house. He found the front door closed. He was locked out. He rang the bell and banged on the door. Eventually Lucy's voice came through the letter-box. 'What?'

'What do you mean – WHAT? Open the bloody door! Oh, you are in so much trouble, kid.' He was aware of being stared at by the woman going past the gate with her dog.

Reluctantly Lucy opened the door. 'Get your clothes on!' ordered Leo. Lucy could tell he was really angry. She presumed the woman had been his ex-wife. What was the big deal, anyway?

Leo got dressed, and five minutes later he and Lucy were in the car.

'You do in fact have your house keys, I take it?' he demanded as he started the engine.

'Yes,' replied Lucy sulkily. She decided she was going off Leo in a big way.

'I trust you realise,' said Leo, as they made their way to South Ken, 'that by your irresponsible behaviour you have caused huge problems for me and for others?'

'Oh, be quiet,' mumbled Lucy. He sounded exactly like the head of sixth form studies the time that someone let off the fire extinguisher outside the common room. He'd be threatening her with detention next.

'What do you suppose Anthea's going to say when she finds out about your little escapade?'

'I don't give a bugger.' She was tired of being told off like some naughty kid. What kind of a bad idea had this been, anyway? She glanced at his hands on the steering wheel, then at the grim set of his jaw, and thought yeah, lovely though he was, he was getting on a bit.

Five minutes later they drew up outside her house. 'OK,' said Leo, leaning over and opening the door for her. 'Off you go.' She looked at him with dark, baleful eyes. Despite the damage she'd unwittingly done, he suddenly felt mildly sorry for her, and her wounded teenage pride. Relenting, he said, 'Look, about last night – I didn't say no because I don't like you. Believe me... You're a sweet girl. Don't take it personally.'

Lucy said nothing – merely got out and slammed the car door.

Her mother was sitting at breakfast in her pyjamas, reading the newspaper. She looked up over her glasses as Lucy came in.

'Hello, darling. You're back early from Georgia's. I hope you girls got a decent night's sleep?'

'Yeah,' sighed Lucy. She went to the fridge and poured herself a glass of orange juice, thinking darkly about what Leo had said. She fully intended to take it personally. What other way was there to take it?

18

Leo drove home, trying to work out what, if anything, to tell Anthea about this bizarre episode. He showered and had breakfast, and decided in the end to tell her nothing. Presumably Lucy's damaged pride would prevent her from saying anything either.

Of more importance was the question of whether Rachel was going to try to use this morning's incident as an excuse to stop him seeing Oliver. He rang Rachel's mobile three times, but each time it was switched to voicemail. In the end he left a terse message to the effect that she had been utterly wrong about the situation at his house, and that he would ring her tomorrow to clear it up. Some hope, he thought, as he clicked his phone off. Whether she believed him or not, she really wanted an excuse to keep Oliver away from him. Why? He couldn't fathom the woman.

He did a few chores, then towards lunchtime sat down at the kitchen table and began to make a list of things he needed to buy. The sliding glass door at the end of the kitchen was open to the September air, and after a few moments, his list neglected, he found himself gazing at the playhouse and swing at the end of the garden, thinking of Oliver. The sense he had of missing him, combined with apprehension that Oliver might not come here again for some time after the events of this morning, weighed depressingly. He sat for a while, conjuring the sound of the little boy's voice in his head, and the sight of him playing in the garden on his last visit.

After lunch he did some desultory shopping, and later in the afternoon Anthony rang. He and Leo had been instructed together in a case which was due to be heard in the middle of next week, and he wanted to go over certain points with Leo.

'Look,' said Leo, 'if you're not busy tomorrow, why don't you come over for a late lunch, and we can spend the afternoon going through everything. Come around half two.'

'Fine. I'll bring the papers and a bottle of wine. By the way,' added Anthony, 'I know you're probably busy, but Chay's making a flying visit from the States and has booked some restaurant in Smithfield for a load of people this evening. He asked me to mention it to you in case you'd like to come along.' Chay Cross, Anthony's father, was a well-known artist of the post-modern persuasion, and Leo was a trustee of the board of a museum of modern art which Chay had established a few years ago in Shoreditch. Leo hesitated – with Oliver due to stay for the weekend, he had cleared Saturday evening. Perhaps he could do with something to take his mind off the problem of Rachel and Oliver, but somehow he didn't feel up to socialising with Tracy Emin and her ilk.

'I don't think so – but thank him. Tell him I'm looking forward to the Diebenkorn retrospective in November and that I hope to see him then.'

'OK, but if you change your mind, just give me a call.'

Leo went through to his study to do a little work to take his mind off things. There were yet more papers in the Humble Construction case to read through, and as he did so he found himself wondering if Brian Bennett had got to the bottom of that double invoice yet.

Outside, as early dusk began to fall, a dark red BMW swung round the corner and slowly cruised the street. Viktor Kroitor peered out of the darkened windows at the house numbers, then told the driver to stop. He stepped out on to the pavement. 'Go round the block until I come out,' he told the driver. As the car pulled away, Viktor stood for a moment surveying Leo's house. Very handsome, he thought, and in a nice part of town. This lawyer must earn a lot of money. Perhaps that was why Sir Dudley thought he couldn't be bribed. In any event, Viktor didn't care for throwing good money away when he had cheaper, often more persuasive means at his disposal. He had learned enough about Leo Davies to know that there were quite a few buttons available to be pushed. He approached the house.

Leo was pouring himself an early evening drink and wondering whether he shouldn't go over to Smithfield after all, when the doorbell rang. He went to answer it. The man who stood on the doorstep was tall, well-built, with dark hair and a stubbly beard and moustache. He was dressed in a black crew-neck sweater and trousers beneath a three-quarters-length tan leather coat, with shoes that matched. The coat and shoes, in Leo's mind, marked him out as Eastern European, and his immediate thought was that this was some tradesman, rather smarter than usual, plying for work in the neighbourhood. But when the man smiled and said, 'Mr Davies?' Leo knew it was something else altogether. Suddenly the big man moved forward, taking Leo entirely off guard, and thrust him back into the hallway. Then he stepped inside, pulling the door shut behind him.

'What the bloody hell are you up to?' demanded Leo. He checked his immediate instinct to respond physically to this intrusion – the man was young, powerfully built, and looked extremely unpleasant – and tried to make sense of the situation. The man knew his name. How? Whatever he was after, he evidently wasn't here to burgle the place – or if he was, he was going about it in an unorthodox manner. He was offering no further violence – on the contrary, he was now simply standing in the hallway, smiling and relaxed, in the manner of someone in complete control. When he spoke, it was in a thick accent, but his English was excellent, grammatical.

'Good evening, Mr Davies. I have come to see you on a matter of business.'

'Was it entirely necessary to force your way in here, in that case?' asked Leo.

Viktor shrugged. 'A small precaution, to make sure of no unpleasant scene on the doorstep. Also to show you how it will be if you are obstructive in this business.' He suddenly frowned.

'Go on, go on!' he said, motioning Leo into the living room.

Once in the room, Viktor glanced round appreciatively, then caught sight of the tumbler of Scotch which Leo had poured for himself. 'Pour me some whisky, too, then we will sit down and talk.'

Leo did as he was told. 'OK,' said Viktor, taking the glass from Leo. 'Sit. We can be civilised.'

Leo sat down in an armchair, his heart thudding, while Viktor made himself comfortable on the sofa, and took a long pull at his Scotch.

'Would you mind telling me what business it is that has you forcing your way into my home? Are you working for someone I know?' Leo knew that his work, involving as it did a number of multi-million dollar cases and any number of possibly fraudulent businessmen and crooked shipowners, had the potential to stretch into areas of criminality, but never in his career had anyone confronted him in this way. He had no idea what the man could possibly want.

Viktor set his glass down and wiped his mouth. 'You are working on a case to do with Humble Construction – yes?' Leo nodded, putting certain pieces together, and realising the man must be Ukrainian. 'And you have started asking questions about a company called Landline.'

Landline – that was the name of the company which had submitted the duplicate invoice for some work to do with furnaces. Leo tried to appear unconcerned, but it was the last thing he felt. 'In a peripheral fashion, I've raised some queries – yes.'

Viktor frowned. 'What is peripheral?'

'Associated. Unimportant, if you like.'

Viktor nodded, and drained his glass. He was silent for a moment, then said conversationally, 'You have a little boy – yes? A very nice little boy. I have seen him coming out of his school. His mother is pretty, too. But she doesn't live here?'

Leo's stomach felt as though it was suddenly twisting in a vicious knot. 'No,' he replied evenly, 'she doesn't live here.' He wanted to kill this man, but he knew that belligerence was the last thing needed here. His job was to listen, like a good lawyer.

'No,' said Viktor, and smiled. 'Actually, I know that. I know where she lives. I know where she works, and I know where your little boy goes to school.' He set his glass down. 'I know everything about you, Mr Davies. Everything I need to know. Strictly personal.'

'Look, what the fuck do you want?' demanded Leo. Mention of Oliver and Rachel had made him suddenly very afraid, and very angry. 'If you've come here to threaten me, or my family, I want to know why.'

'I have told you all you need to know.' Viktor was calm. 'The Landline company – you don't ask any more questions, you don't make any investigations. You leave it alone. It doesn't concern you.' He gave Leo a long, intent look. 'OK? Because otherwise, nasty things could happen to your little boy, and his pretty mother may not end up so pretty. Quite simple.' He indicated his empty glass. 'Very good whisky.' He stood up, his leather coat making a faint creaking noise, and went towards the door. Then he turned and said, 'By the way, they tell me about you barrister people – they say you cannot be bribed. Is this true?'

'Not as a rule,' replied Leo. 'We're not much impressed by threats, either.' Which was as far from the truth as it was possible to get. He just didn't want this bastard to leave him utterly humiliated.

Viktor laughed. Then he came across the room towards Leo, until he was standing very close – so close that Leo could smell the reek of tobacco. 'Mr Davies,' said Viktor softly, 'what kind of man do you think I am? Today's visit has been very civilised, very polite. But I am not a civilised man. Not really. True, I dress nice, I drive a nice car, but – ' he shook his head ' – I am not a nice man. The things I have done to people, you cannot imagine. Not just killing. If I had wanted, I could have shown you what I mean – here, now. But I don't think I need to go so far. You are an intelligent man. So, please – when you hear me talk about your son, and his mother, I beg you – be impressed.'

He turned and left the room without a word, and a few seconds later Leo heard the front door close. He fell into an armchair, shocked, and sat there for some moments, going over everything that had happened in the past five minutes. How much longer than five minutes it had seemed. He felt shaky. He noticed the tumbler of whisky next to his chair, picked it up, and drained it. Then he got up and poured himself another, and paced around the room, still thinking. He went to the window and looked out, but there was no sign of the man.

Should he call the police? That seemed the obvious thing, but what could they do? What did they ever do, these days? Besides, involving them might put Rachel and Oliver in danger – and that was a good enough reason for saying and doing absolutely nothing. He believed that the man who had just left had been entirely sincere in everything he had said. What Leo wanted to know was – why? What exactly had Sir Dudley Humble got himself caught up in?

19

The next day Anthony arrived for lunch with a bottle of wine, as promised, and several files of papers.

'What's for lunch?' asked Anthony, following Leo into the kitchen.

Though he hadn't slept well, Leo was feeling better than he had twelve hours ago. 'Roast chicken, mashed potatoes and broccoli, followed by Bakewell tart.'

'You made Bakewell tart? That sounds homely.'

'I didn't make it. It came from the farmer's market, along with everything else. Comfort food. I need it right now. So far I have had the most appalling weekend. After yesterday I don't think things could get any more surreal.'

Anthony watched as Leo drained and mashed the potatoes. 'Do you want to tell me about it?'

'I'll tell you over lunch. In the meantime, if you want to help, you can pour us both a glass of the exceptionally fine Manzanilla chilling in the fridge, and then take some knives and forks outside. I thought we'd eat in the garden.'

They ate lunch beneath the mulberry tree, and Leo recounted to Anthony the events of the weekend.

'I'll start with the outlandish, and then move on to the bizarre. On Friday night Anthea's little sister, Lucy, rang me from a night club in Soho – or rather her friend did – and asked me to fetch her, as she was somewhat the worse for wear.'

'Why you?' asked Anthony, helping himself to chicken.

'You may well ask. It seemed there was no one else available, and because I didn't want to abandon Anthea's sister in her time of need, I went to Soho and brought her home in a taxi.'

'Here? Was that wise?'

'As things turned out, no. But at the time it looked like there was no alternative – she appeared to have lost her keys, and seemed pretty much out of it. However,' went on Leo, pouring out the wine which Anthony had brought, 'Lucy made a startlingly fast recovery. So much so that, within half an hour of collapsing in my living room, she was making a play for me.'

Anthony laughed. 'Oh, really?'

'Oh, yes, really. Not only that – ' Leo paused and took a sip of the wine. 'This is remarkably good stuff.' He inspected the bottle. 'Puligny-Montrachet two thousand and one? You spoil us, my boy.'

'Not really – it wasn't as expensive as you think. Anyway, since you spent so much time teaching me about wine when we first met, I like to show you your time wasn't wasted.'

Leo smiled. 'None of that time was wasted. You showed such exceptional promise – in every way. It was a pleasure to educate you.'

It gave Anthony a strange pang to hear Leo talk of those times. He wondered how differently things might have turned out if only he'd been less afraid of his own feelings. But Leo was saying, 'I wonder if Oliver will show the same aptitude and interest when he's older. If I'm allowed near him, that is.'

'Why do you say that?'

'Oh – well, I'll come to that later. It's all connected. Where was I?'

'Anthea's sister made a pass at you. Which you – rebuffed?'

'Indeed. Especially since it turned out that she's seventeen and a virgin, and that she'd selected me specially for the honour of deflowering her.'

'My God!'

'Quite. The whole Soho thing had been a set-up. So there I was, with this mixed-up and, I may say, absolutely delectable girl on my hands – here, have some broccoli – whose advances I had managed to resist, and whom I subsequently had to put up for the night in one of the spare rooms. The next morning, while I was upstairs – and this is where Oliver comes in – she went downstairs to make some coffee. The doorbell rang, Lucy went to answer it, and there on the doorstep was Rachel. I'd forgotten that she was going to spend the weekend at some health farm with a girlfriend, and that I'd agreed to have Oliver. That is to say, it had briefly slipped my mind. I wasn't expecting her to arrive first thing, but then again, I don't think she was expecting some Lolita to answer the door clad only in one of my shirts.'

'Oh. Not good.'

Leo inclined his head. 'Not good. She naturally jumped to the wrong, or perhaps the obvious conclusion, depending on how you judge me.'

'None of her business, though, surely?'

'Well, yes and no. She's been giving me a hard time lately about the way she thinks I conduct my private life, saying she doesn't think it's good for Oliver to be around me in case he's tainted by what she evidently sees as my depravity. Which is a load of bollocks, of course. So, refusing to accept my honest explanation for the situation – '

'For which you can't really blame her.'

'Possibly not. Anyhow, she did her stony-faced, self-righteous number and went off with Oliver, and I haven't been able to speak to her since. I think she's going to use the whole episode as an excuse to keep me from seeing Oliver.'

'She wouldn't be so unreasonable.'

'Wouldn't she? She seems determined to exclude me from as much of his life as she can. I don't know why. I don't think I'm a bad father.' His look of bafflement as he said this touched Anthony.

'So, not a great Saturday.'

'It didn't end there – we still have the bizarre part to come. Finish your chicken, and I'll tell you the rest over pudding.'

As they finished lunch, Leo told Anthony about the man who had made his way into the house the previous evening, and what he had said.

'Was that it? Nothing more?'

'That was it. To forget about the existence of this company,

Landline, to make no more investigations – otherwise, he indicated, harm would come to Oliver and Rachel. That was the message, with no explanation beyond it.' Leo took out a packet of small cigars and lit one. He rarely smoked these days, but recalling yesterday evening's events, he felt the need.

'Have you thought about telling the police?'

'Of course. And I've decided against it.'

'Why?'

'Why? Because I don't care about Landline, and I don't frankly care what Sir Dudley Humble has got himself mixed up in. What I care about is the safety of Oliver and Rachel. And if all it takes is to turn a blind eye to some double invoicing, then so be it. Look – I'm acting for Humble in a bog-standard breach of contract suit. I don't need to concern myself about anything that falls beyond the scope of that case – particularly when Ukrainian heavies come knocking on my door telling me it's against my interests to do so.' He tapped the ash from his cigar. 'And don't tell me that's cowardice. It's common sense.'

'I agree,' said Anthony. 'I'd probably do the same in your shoes. But you must be intrigued.'

'Intrigued? Of course I'm intrigued. The man's been fingered for making secret loans to the Labour party – I've heard well-placed rumours that he's due to be questioned under caution in the next few weeks. And his business seems to be on the slide. But I'm putting the whole thing from my mind.'

'Sure, but even doing that carries its own risks.'

'What do you mean?'

'You know what I mean. Look, the most obvious explanation for what's going on is that Landline has been set up as a bogus company to issue invoices for duplicate or non-existent goods and services, as a way of laundering money from the Ukraine via London. Hence the grossly inflated Landline invoice. Landline is either some sort of shell company, or a satellite of Humble Construction, set up expressly for the purpose, and no doubt Sir Dudley is getting a tidy rake-off for his part in facilitating the whole operation. Some half-wit somewhere down the line has allowed the Landline invoice to get mixed up with the Humble Construction papers – '

'And has probably had his ears cut off for his trouble.'

'The point is, Leo – now that you know about it, you can't ignore it, not while you're acting for Sir Dudley. There may be issues relating to the Proceeds Of Crime Act. But I don't need to tell you that.'

Leo sat smoking in silence for a few moments, then at last he said, 'You're right, of course. I've been thinking about it all morning. God knows what kind of money is coming through Landline – drugs money, money from arms sales, organised crime, the lot. If Sir Dudley's involvement were to be exposed, questions as to his beneficence in the matter of party funding would pale into insignificance. Hence the gentleman who called on me last night.' Leo stubbed his cigar out and rubbed his hands wearily over his face.

'And if it ever was to come out, for whatever reason, and you were found to have known about it – '

'An infinitesimal risk, surely. It's one piece of paper.'

'But you and I managed to work out what's going on quickly enough.'

'True – but if it came to it, I'd simply say it didn't cross my mind, or whatever. Oh, for God's sake, no one's going to ask! The risk is purely theoretical. I'm hardly likely to be disbarred because of one dodgy invoice.'

'True. So what it comes down to is a matter of conscience, I suppose.'

'Forget about conscience. What it comes down to is protecting Rachel and Oliver. There is simply no contest. Much as it irks me to take orders from some Ukrainian wearing caramel-coloured shoes, I intend to do exactly what the man said. There's an end of it.' He rose. 'Come on, help me clear this lot up and we'll get down to some work.'

They went to Leo's study and spent an hour or so preparing for Wednesday's hearing. As they tidied the documents away, Anthony remarked, 'It's been a while since you led me in a case.'

'We work well together,' said Leo. He sat, tapping his teeth with his pen as he watched Anthony's long fingers winding pink tape round one of the bundles. Leo's eyes shifted to the younger man's lean, handsome face, his dark, preoccupied eyes. Did anything remain in Anthony's heart, he wondered, of the old intimacy they had once shared? Or was there nothing left but this friendly rapport, an easy disguise for that which had been too much for both of them? He knew now, from the experience of one shared night, that Anthony was not the stuff of casual lovers, like Luca. So what was he? And what could he ever be, now?

'Do you remember,' asked Leo suddenly, 'that evening you came to my house in Oxford, after the cricket match? When you were just a pupil?'

Anthony paused in what he was doing. 'Yes, of course,' he replied quietly. 'I think about it a lot.' The atmosphere, like the early evening light outside the window, had changed subtly. 'Why?'

'I think about it, too.' Leo rose from his chair, taking a volume from the desk and putting it in the bookcase. 'I think we found a moment then – you and I. But we lost the moment, and it never returned.'

'Don't say that. Our relationship's been through some testing times, but it's always survived. Look at us now.'

'Yes.' Leo nodded. 'Look at us now.' Leo stared down at the carpet for a moment then, fixing Anthony with his blue gaze, said, 'Whenever I think of what it would be like to have someone, just one person – you know, there at the end of the day, someone to listen, someone to be with, to share – Oh, I don't know... Whenever I think about that, I find myself thinking of you.' He shrugged. 'So nothing is enough.'

Anthony was silent for a few, astonished seconds, then he murmured, 'God, Leo.' He rose, and went to Leo, and put his arms gently around him. They stood thus for a moment.

Leo moved away, uttering a small, laugh. 'I'm sorry. All that business yesterday must have affected me – '

'Leo, you don't need to make excuses.' Leo had gone over to the window; he stood there, his hands in his pockets, head bowed slightly. Anthony didn't think he had ever seen him look so vulnerable. 'I'm here,' he added. 'You know I am.'

Leo nodded. 'In your fashion. But we can never – ' He stopped, and sighed. 'I have this life, you see. I have this life, and I need to live it a certain way to keep Oliver. Do you understand?'

'Yes,' said Anthony, 'I understand. And it makes no difference.'

'Ah, but it does,' replied Leo. 'It does.' He stood there thoughtfully for a few seconds, then turned abruptly and said, 'Roger spoke to me about this virtual chambers business. He says he's mentioned it to you, too.'

'That's right,' said Anthony, a little thrown by the sudden change of tack.

'And?'

'And what?'

'Will you leave? Will you go and operate in some chamberless limbo, with your clerk at the end of a phone and your briefs winging their way like invisible angels to your inbox?'

Anthony laughed. 'I don't know. I doubt it. It depends.'

'On what?'

Anthony's laughter faded to a smile. 'On you. It depends on you.' Leo looked away. Anthony asked, 'What about you? Would you leave?'

Leo shook his head. 'I have no idea. They only want me for what they call 'prestige'. But there are attractions. Many of them to do with having more time to spend with Oliver.' He turned to face Anthony again. 'I'm sorry – for you it comes down to me, and for me it comes down to Oliver.'

'Don't worry,' replied Anthony. 'That's the way it should be. Just let me know what you decide, will you?' Leo nodded. Anthony gathered up his papers. 'I'd better get going,' he said. 'I have a few things to do at home.'

'Fine.' Leo moved with Anthony towards the study door.

'How was Chay's gathering last night?'

'Good – fairly uproarious, as you can imagine.'

'Perhaps I should have come. At least I'd have been spared my unpleasant visitor. But he'd only have come another time. Tonight. Or tomorrow night.' Leo opened the front door for Anthony.

'Thanks for lunch,' said Anthony.

'Thanks for coming.'

Anthony hesitated, then leaned forward and kissed Leo gently on the cheek. From the doorway Leo watched as Anthony got into his car and drove away.

20

That evening Leo still couldn't reach Rachel either at home or on her mobile. Evidently she was deliberately choosing not to take his calls. He paced from his study to the living room, then through to the kitchen and back again. Darkness was falling outside. His conversation with Anthony had left him with a vague sense of melancholy, and now he could feel his mood deepening to one of anger. How bloody childish, thought Leo. The stupid incident with Lucy might have provided Rachel with the very excuse she'd been looking for, but she couldn't, surely, just cut off all contact with Oliver without further discussion? It wasn't fair on him, or on Oliver. Then again, perhaps this was her way of punishing him for a short while – of showing that she still had some areas of control and power in their relationship. This, he suspected, lay at the heart of it. He knew she still loved him – it was there in her voice and glance, in the effortful frigidity of her manner towards him. She very probably hated and despised herself for what she no doubt regarded as a weakness. So maybe he should just let her inflict her punishment, for however long it lasted.

A thought suddenly struck him, and it was one so awful that he felt it as a physical pain below his ribs. What if the man who had come the previous evening had decided, as a precaution, to make real his threat? He had, after all no way of knowing whether Leo would take him seriously and desist from making further enquiries about Landline. He might have decided to pre-empt any possibility of uncertainty by demonstrating to Leo that he meant what he said. Damn the woman for refusing to answer the phone! The thought, now lodged within his brain, that some harm might be coming to Oliver at this very moment, made him grab his jacket and drive the couple of miles to Rachel's house in Chiswick. But the house was in darkness, and no one answered when he rang and knocked. Her car wasn't in the driveway. She could be anywhere. He simply had no way of knowing whether she and Oliver were safe or not.

There was nothing further he could do. Leo drove home with a feeling of intolerable helplessness. He poured himself a large Scotch, and then remembered that Anthea had flown back from Barbados that day. It wasn't her style to call him, so to take his mind off the plague of troubles which had descended on him, he picked up the phone and rang her.

'Hi,' said Anthea, when she heard his voice. She sounded tired, but in a good mood. 'Have you missed me?'

'Of course,' said Leo. 'Counting the days. How was your trip?'

'Oh, you know – fun in its way. Fantastic weather, but a lot of the usual standing around. And the flight back was delayed by an hour. Still, here I am. What's new with you?'

'Not a lot,' replied Leo, thinking grimly of Lucy, who was responsible for half of this trouble. 'I wondered if you felt like some company this evening? It hasn't been the best of weekends, and I could do with seeing you. I really have missed you.'

'Darling, that's sweet, but to be honest, I'm pretty whacked, and I have an early call. I don't think tonight's a great idea. Why don't you come over tomorrow evening and we'll have supper here? Around half eight?'

'Sounds good. I'll see you then. Sleep tight.'

Leo hung up the phone, finished his drink, then poured himself another one. The hours until he could call Rachel at work tomorrow, and set his mind at rest, were going to be long and slow.

Anthea switched off her phone and gave Lola a smile of triumph.

'Told you. He's been missing me – he said it twice – and he's just longing to see me!'

'Lucky you.' Lola picked up the bottle of white wine and poured them both some more. 'Why did you put him off?'

'Because I genuinely am tired, and because sex with Leo is a lovely, but very exhausting business. And when he wants to see me late in the evening, it's mostly about sex.'

'In that case, you should have let him come over, and we could have had a jolly little threesome together. Take the strain off you.'

Anthea snorted into her wine. 'Darling, you jest! I doubt if that's Leo's scene at all – he may have a fantastic sex drive, but I'd say he's pretty straight in his tastes and inclinations.' She drained her glass. 'Which is the way I like my men, if they're going to be husband material.' She held her glass out. 'Come on, let's have some more. I'll sleep like a baby tonight.'

'So you're really getting serious about him?' asked Lolly, filling Anthea's glass again.

'I could be,' said Anthea, with a faraway look in her eye. 'The question is – could he? He's got some way to go before he's ready, which is why I'm still playing a very long, careful game, darling.'

'I just wish there were more like him,' said Lola wistfully. 'He's such a divine man – I don't just mean to look at. He's good company. He's fun. You lucky bitch.'

'I am rather, aren't I? Just don't like him too much, Lolly. He's pretty much taken, even if he doesn't know it yet.'

21

As soon as he got into chambers the next morning, Leo rang Rachel's office.

'Is Miss Dean in?' he asked the girl on the switchboard.

'I think she's just arrived – who shall I say is calling?'

Leo was swept with relief – his fears, while far from ridiculous, were unfounded. So far, at least. He hesitated, then gave his name. Could she be so petty as to carry on refusing to talk to him? Very possibly.

But a few seconds later Rachel came on the line, sounding distinctly chilly.

'Rachel,' he asked, 'are you and Oliver all right?'

'All right? Of course we are.'

'I just meant – I hope you got home safely.' There was a pause. 'We have to talk. Things were not what they seemed on Saturday.'

'Leo, what I saw wasn't open to many interpretations.'

'Even if that were true, which it's not, it would still be nothing to do with – ' He stopped. An argument on the phone was the last thing he wanted. 'Meet me for lunch.'

'I can't. I'm tied up today.'

'Tomorrow then. It's the only day I can do. I'm in court the rest of the week. We need to talk about this. We can't leave things as they are. It isn't fair to me or Oliver.'

She hesitated for a moment, then said, 'All right.'

'We can meet at that wine bar at the bottom of Fetter Lane. I'll book a table. One o'clock?'

'Don't bother booking anything, Leo. I don't think it's going to be a lengthy meeting.'

'We'll see,' replied Leo, and hung up. He sat back in his chair, thinking. Not for the first time, he found himself debating whether Rachel should be told about the man who had called on Saturday evening, and the threats made against her and Oliver. There was a case for saying that she should be told, since it so closely concerned her. On the other hand – what good would it do? What possible precautions could she take, bar taking Oliver out of school and leaving the country? She'd only go out of her mind with worry. And she would probably just use it as an other excuse for keeping Oliver away from him. He sighed and swivelled round in his chair to stare out of the window. The leaves on the trees in Caper Court were still green, but there was a mellowness in the air which spoke of early autumn. He felt utterly trapped by the situation. What he wanted to be able to do was to demonstrate to these mad Ukrainians that he had no intention of investigating Landline, so that they would back off and leave his family alone. But how? The only thing he could do was what he'd been told to do – precisely nothing. What he would really like would be to get Sir Dudley in here and confront him over the whole stinking business, but that, of course, could spell catastrophe. Leo pondered. There might, however, be some other, more subtle, judicious means of getting his point across... He flipped open his diary. Excellent. He had a conference booked tomorrow at three with Sir Dudley and Brian Bennett, when they were due to go over the skeleton argument. He would do it then.

Towards the end of the day, as he finished the remains of his work, Leo found himself thinking about Anthea. He was genuinely anxious to see her. All he wanted from her was some ordinary human kindness and comfort. He was sorely in need of it.

On his way into the clerks' room to leave some letters, he came upon the tail end of another row between Roger and Maurice.

'Just don't fucking patronise me!' Roger was shouting at Maurice. 'I've had enough of it!' And he pushed past Leo and stormed upstairs.

Felicity, standing by the franking machine, rolled her eyes at Leo.

'Maurice,' said Leo mildly, 'do you think you and Roger could conduct your lovers' tiffs out of range of the reception area? It gives the visitors a bad impression.'

Maurice said nothing, merely glared at Leo and left the clerks' room.

'What the hell was all that about?' Leo asked Felicity.

'I dunno. It started off with some argument about paying for sandwiches, or something, and the next thing Roger was accusing Mr Faber of snooping round looking in his pigeon-hole and his diary. Them two argue about anything. I wish they'd do it upstairs and not in here. Gives me a bleeding headache.' She put out her hand. 'That your post, Mr D? Give it here.'

Leo sighed inwardly. He could sense a rift deepening in chambers. Perhaps the sooner Roger and his merry band went off to operate in cyberspace, the better. The question was – would he join them? He still had no idea. He had no idea about anything, except that he wanted to get out of the building and go to see Anthea.

Anthea opened the door wearing a white, cropped-sleeve top cut above the satin-soft skin of her midriff, blue linen trousers and wedge-heeled sandals. Her skin was lightly tanned from her week in Bermuda, and her freshly-washed blonde hair shone silkily. She looked every inch the model, and perfectly pleased with her own loveliness.

'You are,' said Leo, kissing her, 'a beautiful and refreshing sight.'

She smiled. 'So are you. Nice to know you've missed me.'

He kissed her at length and with even more passion. 'I have missed every single thing about you. It's been a bad few days, and not just because you've been away.'

'Come through and tell me all about it.'

They went through to the living room and Anthea poured Leo a drink. 'No Lucy,' he remarked, glancing round. The last thing he wanted was to see her, but it would have been reassuring to know that Anthea had, and that the danger of her saying anything about the weekend had passed.

'Amazing, isn't it? She usually seems to have some radar that tells her when you're coming round. I think she has a bit of a crush on you. Actually, I haven't seen her since I got back. Maybe she's decided to start doing some work for her A levels for a change.'

'Which school is she at?' asked Leo, keen to skip any reference to Lucy's infatuations.

'Rooker's, over in Knightsbridge. I wish Mummy had sent her to boarding school, the way she did me, then I wouldn't have her coming round here drinking my vodka. I swear to God we never did that kind of thing in my day.'

'In my day.' Leo smiled and came to embrace her. 'You make yourself sound positively ancient.'

'I sometimes positively feel it,' sighed Anthea. 'I look at Lucy and I think oh, to be that age again.'

'I'm very glad you're not,' said Leo, and meant it most sincerely.

Roger, still in a filthy temper, went into Simon's room without knocking. Simon glanced up in surprise from his work.

'Come on,' said Roger abruptly, 'let's go to the pub. I feel like getting rat-arsed.'

'I will in a minute. Just let me finish this.'

Roger pushed his glasses on to the bridge of his nose and sighed, then paced the room, waiting for Simon.

'OK. Done,' said Simon at last. He rose and put on his jacket. 'I can't promise to see you to the ultimate conclusion of your stated ambition, but I'll come part of the way. Where d'you fancy going?'

'Anywhere,' said Roger. 'Anywhere that bastard Faber's not likely to be.'

Eight hours later Roger woke up, uncertain about many things –

where he was, what time it was, and how much he'd had to drink. It took him more than a few seconds to work out the answers – at his desk in chambers, at quarter past one in the morning, and a lot. He leaned back and groaned. His reading lamp was on. How had he ended up asleep at his desk? He remembered leaving The Devereux with Simon and Rory and that chap Timothy from 20 Essex Street around half eight, then Rory had gone home, and he and the other two had gone to The George, then Simon and gone home and it had just been him and Timothy. The last thing he remembered was coming back to chambers at the end of the evening to get something. Sleep, apparently. He recalled passing Stephen's half-opened door and seeing Stephen working late, but he hadn't gone in. He must have come upstairs and sat down, and fallen asleep. He'd been asleep for over three hours, he reckoned, and he didn't exactly feel rested and refreshed.

'Oh God...' muttered Roger, getting unsteadily to his feet. He still felt pretty pissed, his mouth was dry and his head aching. What he needed was some paracetamol and a large glass of water. Where to get them? He went out to the landing and snapped on the light. Everywhere was totally silent. Perhaps the secretaries kept some in that cupboard above the fridge in the little kitchen. He went along the corridor to the kitchen, found no paracetamol, and decided to make himself a cup of black coffee instead. As he waited for the kettle to boil, it occurred to Roger that he wasn't going to be able to get out of the building without setting the alarm off, since obviously everyone else had gone home hours ago. He recalled that on the top floor there was a bed and a shower room, which they kept for untold emergencies; he would just have to kip there.

As he made his way along the corridor with his mug of coffee, Roger passed Maurice's room. His eye caught the faintest of glows through the half-open door. Surely Maurice wasn't still here? Cautiously he nudged the door open. The room was in darkness, except for the tiny glow of Maurice's laptop, which had been left switched on. Roger went in and sat down at the desk, putting his coffee mug down carefully. Maurice's laptop – what a gift. Presumably no chance of getting into its dark secrets without a password, though. He tapped the touch pad and the screen blinked into full life. Good God – for some reason Maurice had stopped in the middle of looking something up and just left it on. What Roger was looking at was the page from some judgment or other. No need for passwords. He was already in.

Now fully awake and feeling a lot better, Roger closed the document on the screen. Not quite certain what he was looking for, he dipped in and out of various files, fishing around, telling himself what he was doing was no worse than the way Maurice snooped through Roger's diary. At length he came across a folder named 'INV3' and opened it. He began to read the documents contained within the file, hardly able to believe what he had found. They were fee notes raised by Maurice, addressed to various companies and individuals, and all requesting payment directly to Maurice Faber for work done. Direct billing, cutting out the clerks, taking away their percentage – the one thing which no barrister was permitted to do. On a quick calculation, Maurice was billing directly for his services to the tune of tens of thousands.

'Well, well, you cheeky bastard,' murmured Roger. No wonder Maurice's billing figures were down. The money was going straight into his pocket, and by-passing chambers.

With a wondering smile, Roger continued to trawl Maurice's computer for another three quarters of an hour, taking occasional sips of his coffee. Not only did he find further damning invoices and emails, he also found the confidential reference which Maurice had written on behalf of Melanie, Roger's friend, the erstwhile pupil who had rebuffed Maurice's advances some months ago. Roger read it, and as he did so, any guilt he might have felt at prying into Maurice's computer vanished instantly and entirely. No wonder Melanie was finding it hard to get a job. Some of the things Maurice had written were downright lies. What a shit he was, taking his petty revenge in this way.

Roger tapped a few keys and sent a copy of the reference winging its way to his own computer, where he would be able to print it out tomorrow and show it to Melanie. Quite what she would be able to do about it, he wasn't yet sure. As for the incriminating invoices and emails — Roger reflected for a moment as to how best to deal with these. At length he decided. He opened an email, wittily headed it 'Oops, look what's on my hard drive!', and attached to it each incriminating fee note and email from Maurice's folder. The he clicked on Maurice's address book, highlighted the name of every member of chambers, including the clerks, and with a broad smile of satisfaction and not a moment's hesitation, clicked 'Send to all.'

22

Sir Dudley, who had been brooding unhappily for some time over the matter of the Landline document which Leo had turned up, rang Viktor Kroitor for reassurance.

'I'm seeing Davies with my solicitor tomorrow. I need to know where we stand. I hope you've managed to put a lid on this?'

'It's taken care of.'

'Well, what d'you mean by that? What's been done? I need to know! Have you managed to get hold of the bloody invoice, or what?'

'No need. The invoice was never the problem. The problem was Mr Davies, and I've attended to him.'

'What the hell d'you mean – you've attended to him? What the fuck's been happening, Viktor? If you've made matters worse – '

'I paid him a visit,' said Viktor.

'You stupid sod! If that's a euphemism for strong-arm tactics – '

'I talked to him at the weekend, that's all. I persuaded him it would be best for him, and his nice little son and the little boy's mother, if he forgets all about the invoice, and asks no further questions.'

'You threatened him? For Christ's sake, Viktor, are you mad? What if he calls in the police?'

'I don't think he will.'

'Think? When did you ever do any thinking, you brainless Ukrainian shit! My God, it's bad enough that I already have the police on my back – '

'What?' asked Viktor sharply. 'What is it with the police?' He had not overlooked Sir Dudley's insult; he had coolly stored it away, together with a number of other slights and affronts handed out by Sir Dudley in the course of their relationship, against the day when payment became due.

'Nothing that concerns you. It's a minor political thing. I'm more worried about what Davies will do now. He's bound to link your visit to me. What the hell are you doing in London, anyway? You didn't tell me you were coming.'

'I had business to attend to.'

'My God, this could be turning into a disaster.... What did Davies say when you spoke to him? You didn't harm him, did you?'

'I did not touch him. He said very little. He listened, which is what I wanted him to do. I frightened him, which is also what I wanted. I didn't have to do much. Why do you think he should care about your stupid invoice? What makes you think he is interested in finding out what is going on?'

Sir Dudley sighed heavily. 'I don't know. It's just the thought of anyone – I mean, my God! My God, Viktor!'

Viktor had long thought that Sir Dudley had not really the right temperament for this business. He could wish they had chosen someone less panicky and paranoid. In the end, Sir Dudley was more likely than anyone to wreck everything. That much was becoming clear.

'Calm yourself. He won't do anything, and he won't ask any more questions. He's not interested. I told him to forget all about the invoice, and I think he will.'

'I bloody well hope you're right, Viktor. I bloody well hope you're right.' Sir Dudley ended the call, wondering how on earth he was going to play things at his next meeting with Davies.

23

Leo decided to work at home the following morning on an up-and-coming House of Lords appeal. There was no need to go into town until his lunchtime appointment with Rachel. He sat in his study with the window open to the sights and scents of early September, and reflected that there was something to be said for getting down to work every morning without having to shave and put a suit and tie on. Maybe if he were to join Roger and the others in their virtual chambers, it would be a persuasive factor with Rachel in allowing him more contact with Oliver. Presumably she'd rather he was with his father than a child-minder. Or would she? He'd find out the answer to that in a couple of hours' time.

Lunch with Rachel was never going to be easy. Leo knew she would arrive in a resistant frame of mind, expecting him to pitch into explanations and excuses, which she could then rebuff from her higher moral ground. He decided to subvert her expectations. He got there slightly ahead of time and ordered a bottle of white Burgundy, even though he knew she rarely drank at lunchtime, a plate of rare roast beef and salad for himself, and a dish of smoked salmon and new potato salad for her, which he knew she liked.

'You're looking very pretty,' he said, when she arrived. And she was. Her dark hair was loose, soft and shining, and she was wearing a close-fitting grey dress and a smart, boxy little black jacket. She accepted the compliment with the faintest of smiles, as Leo pulled her chair out for her, and she sat down. He could tell she was tense, ready to fight her corner. He had already poured her a glass of wine, knowing she would refuse one otherwise. He raised his own glass. 'Happy birthday.

Tomorrow, isn't it?'

She nodded, and took a sip of her wine. 'Thanks.'

'If you'd got here two minutes earlier,' he remarked, 'you'd have had the pleasure of seeing your old friend Eddie Stamapoulos.' Leo gestured towards the depths of the wine bar. 'He's just gone through to the back.'

Rachel immediately forgot her froideur. 'Really?' Leo knew this would get her – Eddie was a charming Greek fraudster who had been the bane of her life in a series of cases a few years ago, and for whom she had a love-hate regard. She glanced over her shoulder, as if to catch a glimpse. 'I wonder when they let him out.'

'God knows. He looked as smiling and confident as ever, lunching with two City punters whom he's probably going to take to the cleaners any day soon. What was that case you had with him, the one involving the steel cargo?'

'*The Mimeris*. That was the one where he sold the same steel cargo five times to different people – ' She stopped, suddenly remembering her role and the way she had intended to behave. At that moment the waitress, previously primed by Leo as to the timing, brought their food.

'I ordered for you,' said Leo. 'I knew you didn't want to hang around.'

'Thank you,' said Rachel, a little disarmed. She waited till the waitress had gone, then picked up her fork and ate a sliver of smoked salmon.

'I remember when you were pregnant with Oliver, how you insisted on eating smoked salmon for supper every evening for an entire fortnight.'

Leo could tell that the recollection touched Rachel, and yet at the same time irked her. He knew exactly why. Any reflection of tenderness on his part was bound to upset her. He knew her mind so intimately that every response was predictable. Was it unkind of him to capitalise on that predictability? He had no idea. It was just the way it was.

She put down her fork and took another sip of wine. 'Leo, don't do this, please.'

'Do what?'

To his alarm, her eyes suddenly grew bright with incipient tears. She looked down quickly, trying to hide the fact. He waited to hear what she would say next.

Eventually, more composed, she said, 'We didn't come here to rake over old times, did we? We came here to talk about Oliver.'

He could still see the distress in her eyes, and it stung him to frankness. 'I'm sorry. I was manoeuvring. I wanted you to be the one to bring up the subject. I thought it would give me some kind of advantage.'

'Well, that's honest. And no, it won't. However, since the subject has come up, I'll let you be the first to deal with it.'

Leo began to eat his lunch, allowing himself a few moments' reflection. 'I don't have a lot to say, really. First and foremost, I want to be able to see Oliver – soon. Secondly, and much less important, the explanation I gave you when you came round on Sunday is true. The girl who answered the door is called Lucy, she's the sister of the woman I'm seeing – Anthea – and she was there because I'd rescued her, drunk, from some Soho night-club. I'm not the kind of man who sleeps with his girlfriend's teenage sister.'

Rachel gave a short laugh. 'Oh yes, you are, Leo. That's exactly the kind of man you are.' All traces of pain and defen-siveness had disappeared.

He shrugged. 'What can I do? You're utterly determined to believe what you want. I can only reiterate – the silly kid got drunk, and I had to help. Either way, it's no reason to keep Oliver from me. I hope you'll let him come to me this weekend, as usual.'

She shook her head, her expression withdrawn, closed, and took a couple of mouthfuls of wine.

Leo put down his knife and fork. 'What does that mean? Is that a no?' Silence. He studied Rachel's face, then he asked abruptly, 'What is it, Rachel? What *really* is it? Do you think I'm neglectful of Oliver, that I don't care about him?'

She shook her head.

'So why are you deliberately using an pretext to make out that my private life is a problem? Why are you trying to find an excuse to keep him from me?'

Rachel put her elbows on the table, and her hands over her face. Was she crying? Leo couldn't tell. He hoped not. The last thing he wanted was an emotional squall here in the wine bar. Well, if he got one it was probably all his own fault. He had come here intending to keep things relaxed and unemotional, and had achieved exactly the opposite.

After a few moments Rachel uncovered her face; there were no tears, but her expression was weary, distraught. 'Very well – I'll tell you the truth.' She took another sip of wine, struggling with the words she wanted – or didn't want – to say. 'I find it very hard, Leo – seeing you, being with you. I know we should be civilised parents, doing the best for our son, but the fact is – I can't stand to see you. And every time I have to drop him off, or you come to pick him up, I have to pretend it's all fine, when it's not.'

'My God – do you hate me that much?'

She gave a painful laugh. 'No, Leo. I don't *like* you, but it's not the same. I have plenty of reasons not to like you – to despise you, even – but somehow they don't all add up to hate. Quite the opposite. That's the tragedy.' She took a deep breath. 'I need excuses to keep Oliver away, so that I don't have to see you. Because it hurts so much.'

There was a long silence. Then at last Leo said, 'I'm sorry. I'm sorry if it's hard for you. But for Oliver's sake you mustn't let your feelings cloud the issue. Oliver's the important one here. He needs his father.'

'I just can't stand to know that you might have your lovers around when Oliver's there – this Anthea person, for instance, whoever she is – '

'Oliver's never met Anthea,' interrupted Leo. 'Besides, it's a ridiculous thing to say. I didn't raise any objection when you decided to take Oliver and go to live with Charles Beecham after

117

we split up. I didn't go around accusing you of endangering our son's morals. And what about Anthony? I didn't day a word, even though he was probably seeing more of Oliver than I was. Look, Rachel, Oliver's my son, and I have a right to see him, and to live my life as I see fit. We have to be allowed to get on with our separate lives, without blame or animosity.'

'I suppose you're right,' said Rachel, her voice a little shaky.

Leo let out a sigh. 'I still don't understand why you didn't stay with Charles. God knows he loved you enough.'

Rachel stared at her glass. 'I discovered it's not enough to be loved. Then again – ' She looked up at Leo. ' – it's not enough to love, either. Is it?'

'That perfect balance is almost impossible to find.'

'What about you and Anthea? Do you have it?' asked Rachel, her voice edgy.

'I'm not in love with anyone, Rachel. The most important person in my life is Oliver – and you, believe it or not, come a close second.'

'Only as the mother of your son.'

'Don't make it sound inconsequential.' He leaned forward and touched her hand lightly. 'You and I, whatever else went wrong between us, have a child. That means we still have important work to do together, and I want us to do it as amicably as we can. We've got a lot of sports days and parents' evenings ahead of us. Whatever else happens in our lives, the fact of Oliver will always keep us together. Won't you let that be enough?'

The touch of his hand was almost unbearable for Rachel. The fact was, what she really wanted was never to have to see Leo again, because that way the pain would diminish in time. But he was right – she had no real reason or excuse to prevent Oliver from seeing his father, and that meant it would all go on and on. She would have to accept it.

'Yes,' she said at last. 'I know you want the best for him.'

'Then can I see him this weekend?'

'I was taking him to see friends in Hampshire.'

'Sunday, then?'

She nodded, bemused. It always came to this – he was so good, so persuasive, that he always got what he wanted. Which was why he was such a brilliant lawyer. Leo would find an advantageous position in every situation.

He took his hand from hers and went on, 'I might try to work from home more often, so that I can pick Ollie up from school occasionally. In fact, I thought I might try to do that tomorrow, if I can get away. Believe me, I want to be as big a part of his life as I can.'

She gave a weak smile. 'I thought you didn't like him being called Ollie.'

'Sometimes it seems to suit him – particularly in his more unruly moments.'

There was a silence, then Leo said, 'Look, let's for God's sake try to be friends. When we meet, when you come to drop him off or I to pick him up, let's not have any more rancour or hostility, OK?' Rachel sipped her wine and said nothing, but her silence spoke assent. Leo added, 'There's simply no basis for that in our relationship any more.'

No, thought Rachel sadly, there was no basis for any kind of emotion, and that was the problem. Her problem.

24

When he left Rachel, Leo headed off to chambers pretty much unprepared for the drama which had been unfolding there throughout the morning. The little he learned came from Michael Gibbon, whom he met coming in the opposite direction through Serjeant's Inn.

'Leo! Where have you been all morning?'

'Working from home. Why?'

'Felicity's been trying to get hold of you, but apparently your phone's switched off.'

'Bugger.' Leo reached into his pocket for his phone and switched it on. 'I didn't want to be interrupted. What's going on?'

'I'm in a hell of a hurry and I can't really stop, but it's to do with Maurice. Read your emails. I'll talk to you at the end of the day.' And he hurried off towards Fleet Street.

When he reached chambers, Leo went straight to the clerks' room. Apart from Felicity, Henry and Peter, who were all busy on the phones, there was no one else about, and the atmosphere was one of business as usual. Just as he was about to turn and go upstairs to his room, he saw Felicity signalling frantically to him to wait. When she got off the phone she bustled over, bosom heaving in agitation, eyes bright with angry excitement.

'Mr Davies, have you read your emails yet?'

'I've only just come in. I passed Michael outside and he said you'd been trying to reach me. What's going on?'

'Nobody knows – that's just it! We all came in this morning and found a load of emails from Maurice Faber's computer, and they're all fee notes he's been sending out for work done. He's been billing clients direct!'

'This all sounds extremely strange. What has he got to say about it?'

'He's more bothered about the fact that someone's got into his computer. He's all like – My God, there's a hacker in our midst! Something must be done about it!'

Henry came over. 'It's not very good, Mr Davies. Someone's got into the system and has been downloading confidential information from Mr Faber's laptop, and sending it all round the building.'

'See?' exclaimed Felicity. 'Nobody seems to have their priorities right here! Why is nobody bothered about his direct billing?'

'Keep your voice down, Felicity,' said Henry. 'We can't speculate about the content of confidential files at this point.'

'Can't we? I bloody can! No wonder his figures are down.'

'Calm down, Felicity,' said Leo. 'Henry's right. The most important thing is to find out how someone got into Maurice's computer. If it's the work of an outside hacker, then we have a serious problem on our hands, particularly from the point of client confidentiality. Is it just Maurice's computer, or is anyone else affected?'

'Just Mr Faber, so far as we can tell,' replied Henry. 'Peter spoke to the computer people earlier and they're coming over to have a look.' At that moment Peter Weir finished his phone conversation, and came over to join them.

'The computer gurus say it's unlikely to be an external hacker. They said if anyone wanted to download confidential information from our system they would just do it – they wouldn't broadcast the fact to the entire world. Anyway, apparently our system's incredibly well protected, and it's unlikely anyone outside would be able to get into it. They can't be sure, obviously, but they did suggest from the sound of it that someone in chambers could be mischief-making.'

'All right,' said Leo. 'Just carry on for the time being. I'll go and have a word with Maurice.'

Leo went up to his room and switched on his own laptop. He read the emails and inspected the fee notes cursorily. They did appear to show that Maurice had been billing clients directly, but there could be an explanation. He read, too, the emails from Maurice to third parties chasing up payment of sums due. Strange.

He went to Maurice's room and found him on the phone, apparently in a state of some agitation. He waved Leo to a seat.

'Yes,' Maurice was saying, 'I want this investigated as speedily as possible. Yes. Yes, thank you.' He put down the phone. 'Have you seen what's been going on?'

Leo nodded. 'Someone's got into the system. Why just your laptop?'

'That is exactly what I intend to find out. I was speaking to the Met just now. They're going to send someone over.'

'You want to involve the police? Why?'

'Why? Because this is a serious breach of computer confidentiality, Leo! You, as head of chambers, should be the first to appreciate that. I intend to have every member of chambers finger-printed, and issued with a copy of The Misuse Of Computers Act. If I find out it was someone inside this building – '

'Slow down, Maurice,' said Leo. 'Peter's already spoken to the IT people. They say it's unlikely to be someone from outside. They're going to have a look, but they seem to think whoever did this did it from within chambers.'

'All the more reason for a thorough investigation. I am absolutely livid that this has happened – as you should be!'

'Well, I'm startled, yes – ' It occurred to Leo to touch upon the matter of the direct billing which Maurice had apparently been doing, but he decided that perhaps now was not the moment. ' – but I'd rather we tried to sort the matter out ourselves, before involving the police. I think that's the more obvious way to go about things. There's enough bad feeling in chambers without the police finger-printing everyone in sight. Don't you think?'

'No, I can't say I agree with you. I think – '

Leo interrupted him. 'I know what you think, Maurice, but as head of chambers, I want this handled internally, if possible – initially, at any rate. So call the Met and tell them that there is no need for them to look into the matter just yet.' Maurice's dark brows drew together in an angry frown. He seemed about to protest, but Leo said firmly, 'Now. Please.'

Maurice hesitated. He couldn't ignore Leo's authority. 'Very well,' he muttered, and picked up the phone.

After he had made the call, Leo rose. 'Thank you. Let's see if we can't sort this out on our own.' As he reached the door, Leo turned and added, 'By the way, I think there are other matters arising out of this incident which need to be discussed. Such as the content of the documents. But we'll come to that in good time.'

Leo went back to his room to ponder the matter. He suspected that Maurice's outraged demand that the police be brought in was probably mere bluster on Maurice's part, a way of obfuscating the issue of the embarrassing nature of the documents disclosed. He sat down at his laptop and re-read them. It was pretty clear that the paramount motive for disseminating Maurice's private files had been to make trouble for Maurice. He wondered who was responsible, and how they'd managed it. Someone with a grudge against Maurice, and a juvenile sense of humour.

He glanced at his watch. Twenty to three. Sir Dudley would be here with his solicitor in twenty minutes, and that was enough to worry about. Life, at the moment, seemed to be just one damned thing after another.

25

Sir Dudley arrived early for the conference, and was obliged to wait. He sat down on one of the squashy leather sofas in the reception area and tried to read a copy of *Lloyd's List*, but found himself unable to concentrate. He got up and paced around, scanning the spines of the *All England Law Reports* lining the bookshelves, anxiously wondering how Davies would behave towards him when they met. After all, some bloody Ukrainian strong-arm man had gone to his home and threatened him about an invoice which had turned up in Sir Dudley's papers, making the connection obvious, the inference inescapable. That fool Viktor might well have made things worse by going to see Davies. These bloody barristers were so fastidious and above-board, that was the trouble. Then again, Viktor knew what he was doing. He could be an extremely unpleasant man. Leo Davies was probably so frightened that he would do exactly as he had been told. It was just going to be somewhat uncomfortable having to look the man in the eye. Had this case not been worth several hundred thousand, he might have been tempted to pack it in.

A moment later Brian Bennett came into the reception area. Sir Dudley had spoken to Bennett twice in the past week, and on neither occasion had the Landline invoice been mentioned, and his manner as he greeted Sir Dudley now was cheerful and unconcerned. So Davies had said nothing to him, which was good.

The two of them went upstairs to Leo's room. If Sir Dudley had expected some change in Leo's demeanour, he found none. Leo was courteous and businesslike, and his expression as he spoke to Sir Dudley betrayed nothing. They got down to business quickly, going over the main points of the skeleton argument and clarifying peripheral issues. Sir Dudley began to feel confident that the matter of the double invoice had been safely put to rest. He might not like Viktor's methods, or consider them entirely appropriate, but evidently they worked.

Leo, in considering how he would handle the money-laundering issue, had been perfectly prepared to speak in front of Brian, if necessary. At one point in the conference, however, Brian fortuitously excused himself to go to the loo, giving Leo the opportunity to speak privately. After Brian had left the room, a silence fell. Alone with Leo, Sir Dudley suddenly felt acutely conscious of the unspoken issues between them. He began to wonder if the silence would last until Brian returned, but eventually Leo spoke.

'Sir Dudley, I feel obliged to tell you that I had a visitor on Saturday night. An unexpected visitor.'

Sir Dudley stiffened. 'Oh?'

'I don't know the man's identity. He didn't give his name, and I didn't ask for it.' Leo sat back in his chair, his cool blue eyes fastened on Sir Dudley's square, beefy face. 'He came to see me about a document – to be precise, he came about the Landline invoice which turned up recently in the papers relating to this case.' Sir Dudley said nothing, but made an uneasy, frowning effort to convey the impression that the relevance of all this eluded him. Leo let another brief silence elapse before speaking again. 'You must understand, Sir Dudley, that I have certain professional obligations – obligations relating to the Proceeds of Crime Act – '

'I haven't the least idea what you're talking about, Davies. What crime are you referring to? Come to the point.'

'It's just that the natural inference to be drawn from the double invoicing is that there may be some issue concerning money-laundering.' Anticipating Sir Dudley's reaction, Leo added with a polite smile, 'I'm sure it's nothing of the sort, naturally, but given my professional obligations I have to raise the point. Can you confirm to me that nothing of that kind is involved?'

'An absolutely scandalous suggestion! No, of course there isn't!' blustered Sir Dudley. 'I find it quite – '

'That's fine,' interrupted Leo mildly. 'I merely required your assurance. Now that I have it, please forget I ever raised the subject.' The door opened. 'Ah, Brian – Sir Dudley was just enlightening me on the matter of that apparent double invoice. You remember – the one relating to furnace linings? It seems it was raised by mistake, so we needn't worry about it. Now, would anyone like another cup of coffee before we get on?'

Sir Dudley and Brian left Caper Court around five. Brian took a taxi back to his office, and Sir Dudley, now in an extremely disturbed frame of mind, walked across Middle Temple Lane and into Fountain Court. There he switched on his mobile and rang Viktor, pacing up and down beneath the trees beside the splashing waters of the fountain as he waited for Viktor to answer.

Viktor was sitting in the Bayswater hotel, trying to deal with a couple of issues to do with the girls, when his phone rang. He flipped it open, saw who was calling, and sighed as he answered. 'What is it now?'

'I've just come out of a meeting with Davies. He knows what's going on.'

'Of course he knows. He's not a stupid man.' Viktor stubbed out his cigarette, and beckoned one of the girls over. Her face was pasty and her eyes looked bloodshot and heavy. She had been crying, and she was shivering all over. She definitely looked sick; he didn't think she was trying it on.

'Well, don't sound so fucking complacent, man!'

'*Complays*ent?' Viktor guessed this meant what it sounded like it meant. 'Are you're asking – why am I not worried? I don't know, Dudley. Should I be? What did he say?'

'He said – well, he asked if there was anything of a criminal nature that he should know about. The double invoices made him think there could be. He specifically mentioned money-laundering!'

'And you said?' Viktor considered the shivering, sweating girl. They'd have to get a doctor, but one who would keep his mouth shut for the right money.

'I said no, of course!'

'And *he* said?'

'He said – he said that was fine. That nothing more need be said about it.'

'There you are.' He motioned the girl away and lit another cigarette. 'What your clever Mr Davies was doing was telling you that he knows what's going on, but that because he has listened to me, he will do nothing. Don't you see?'

'See? All I fucking well see, Viktor, is that a Queen's Counsel knows that I'm involved in money-laundering! God alone knows what will happen now!'

'Nothing will happen. He has told you that. I'm telling you that.'

'Look, Viktor, it won't do!' Sir Dudley's voice was panicky, urgent. 'It simply won't do. I want you to shut him up – properly.'

'Yesterday you were worried I might have beaten him up! What are you asking now?'

'Viktor, I want this sorted! You do as I say, remember, or you may find yourself without anyone to handle your business in future. I'm warning you! You make damn sure he doesn't say anything!'

Sir Dudley snapped his phone off, and found his palms were damp, his chest heaving. Why had he ever asked Viktor to do anything about the business of the double invoice? It would probably just have gone away in the long run, if he'd let it. Now, however, it was too late.

In the hotel, Viktor switched off his phone. Maybe it would be an idea just to remind Leo Davies that the threat had been real. Nothing heavy – just a little frightener. He looked over at Marko.

'Hey, who was that doctor we got last time? Is he still good? OK, call him.' He indicated the girl. 'Get her out of here for now.' He stood up. 'I think,' he said with a smile, 'that I'll go next door and pay Irina a visit. I haven't seen her since that first day. I'm sure she'd like another chance to show me how grateful she is for bringing her to England.'

'Maybe that's not a good idea, boss,' said Marko awkwardly. 'She might be sick, too. She wasn't looking too good this morning.'

'Don't worry, Marko,' laughed Viktor as he left the room. 'I'll give her something to make her feel better.'

26

After Brian and Sir Dudley had left, Leo sat brooding. He was far from sure that he'd done the right thing in speaking as he had. He had to acknowledge now that his motives went far beyond conveying to Sir Dudley and his henchman that he had no intention of pursuing the matter of the Landline invoice, in the guise of professional protocol. He had needed, as a matter of pride, to show how much he knew, and to demonstrate that matters were not entirely out of his control. Sheer hubris. Christ, what if he had further endangered Oliver or Rachel? Surely not. Uneasy and in need of reassurance, he went to seek out Anthony in his room, and told him what had happened.

'You did the right thing,' said Anthony. 'You had to ask the question, as a matter of professional obligation – '

'Oh, sod professional obligation. I'm only interested in protecting Oliver and Rachel, and I now find myself thinking I might have achieved the opposite. All because I wanted to let that bastard Humble know that I knew what he was up to. What was the point in that?'

'Seriously, Leo – it needed to be said. You've covered your back.'

'Oh, have I really? I wonder.' He paced the room, then sighed. 'Anyway, it's done now.' He moved to the window, and stared out for a few moments. Then he turned and asked, 'On another topic, what do you make of this business with Maurice and his emails?'

'I frankly couldn't believe it,' replied Anthony. He leant forward and tapped at his keyboard, bringing up the incriminating documents. 'Have you spoken to him yet?'

'I've spoken to him, yes, but the only thing he seems willing to discuss right now is the burning topic of computer confidentiality. He wanted to involve the police, but I told him in no uncertain terms that I wanted to contain this and deal with it internally, if possible.'

At that moment there was a rap on Anthony's door, and Peter Weir appeared. 'Mr Davies, can I have a word?'

'Sure.'

'I've got Ray from the computer consultants downstairs. He's done a complete check of the system, and says he's a hundred per cent certain that no one's been hacking in externally. So far as he can tell, someone in chambers has gone into Mr Faber's computer and sent out stuff to everyone in the building.'

'I see. Well, at least we know it wasn't a security breach on a wider scale. No way of telling who it was, I don't suppose?'

'Well, actually – it seems that there is some indication. The documents were sent to everyone's computer, but the only person to whose computer they were actually downloaded is Mr Fry's.'

'Ah.'

'Of course, that doesn't necessarily – '

'No, no. OK. Thanks, Peter.'

Peter left, and Anthony glanced significantly at Leo. 'Surprised?'

'Nope. I'd like to know how he did it, though. I'd better speak to him before things go any further.'

Leo went back to his room, rang Roger and asked to see him. A few minutes later Roger appeared, looking his usual unkempt self, and wearing an expression of disingenuous, enquiring innocence.

'Sit down, Roger. I want to ask you about the matter of Maurice's emails being sent round chambers. It appears it was the work of an insider. Now, I have been asking myself who has enough of a grudge against Maurice to do such a thing, and I have come up with your name. Are you surprised?'

Roger shrugged. 'I'd have thought it's a matter of general interest that Maurice has been billing direct.'

'Maybe so. But I have to ask you if you were responsible –

and before you answer, I should tell you that the documents were found downloaded to your computer, and no one else's.'

Roger didn't seem surprised. 'OK. I was here late last night, a bit hungover, and I came across Maurice's laptop. He'd left it switched on. It was the ideal opportunity to have a little look-see.'

'But what on earth did you think you were doing? You can't just go into people's private – '

'I'll tell you what I was doing.' Roger reached into his pocket and produced a piece of paper. He handed it to Leo. 'It wasn't just a fishing expedition. I specifically wanted to find this. And I did. The rest is incidental, if not without its interest.'

Leo found he was reading a copy of the confidential reference written by Maurice about Melanie. 'I sent a copy to Melanie,' went on Roger, 'because I think it's only fair she should see the lies written about her. I would say there's an issue of defamation here, wouldn't you say?'

Leo groaned. 'Oh, my Lord...' He put the reference down and shook his head.

'I don't know what to say. Except that you have behaved like a first class imbecile.'

'I know,' Roger sighed. 'Nevertheless – '

'Nevertheless, there are certain aspects to this which bear further scrutiny. The point is, you're going to have to put your hand up to this, apologise to Maurice – and then we shall deal with the rest. I'll call a chambers' meeting later this week.'

'What about Melanie's reference?'

'I'll have to speak privately to Maurice about that. There's something in the defamation point.' Roger rose. 'But before you go,' added Leo, 'I want you to promise me that you'll never, ever do anything like this again. We nearly finished up with the police in here.'

'The police?'

'Maurice went ballistic when he found out what had happened. We're lucky we didn't finish up having DNA swabs taken, the way he was carrying on.'

Roger grinned. 'I'd say he has something to hide, then – wouldn't you?'

I need a drink, thought Leo, as Roger closed the door behind him. Time to hunt down Michael, crack a bottle or two in the comforting depths of El Vino's, and discuss it all. After all, in a month or so, it might fall to Michael to take on the mantle of head of chambers and preside over the weird and wonderful world of 5 Caper Court.

27

Lucy came round to Anthea's flat after school and let herself in, Georgia in tow.

'What d'you fancy to eat?' she asked Georgia.

'What is there?'

'Dunno. Let's see.' Lucy slipped off her pumps and padded into the kitchen, raking her fingers through her hair. She opened the fridge, and saw nothing except for a shrivelled red pepper, some pro-biotic yoghurt crap, and a bag of bean sprouts a week past their sell-by date. She hauled out the bottle of vodka – bugger, it was brand new and unopened.

Georgia had followed her into the kitchen. 'What is there? I'm, like, *so* hungry.' She peered into the fridge over Lucy's shoulder. 'My God, what do models live on? No wonder your sister's so thin. I could never be one. I love food too much.'

Lucy shut the fridge door, bringing the vodka with her. 'I could never be one either – I'm the wrong height and I've got a face like a hamster.'

'You've got an adorable face, you know you have. Anyway, that never stopped Peaches Geldof.'

'She's not a model.'

'No, but she gets her photo everywhere. Helps if you're a sado, though.'

'What – like an emo?'

'No, you know – s-a-d-o, sons-and-daughters-of?'

'Oh, my God, yeah – *that* crowd. I really can't stand them. Just 'cause their parents are famous wrinklies from the seventies. It's so sickening.'

'And like, all that stuff they do? Getting little parts in films, and painting and writing rubbish articles? Everyone *knows* it's because of who their dad is. It's not like they've got any real talent, but they're all like, look at me, I'm so fabulous!'

'I know – ticking off all the credential boxes. Makes you want to puke.' Lucy was cruising the kitchen, opening cupboards in search of food. She noticed a white cardboard box lying on the worktop, and stopped. 'Look, Georgie – doesn't that just scream CAKE at you?'

'Ohmigod, it so does...' Georgie lifted the lid. 'Oh, yummy!' Nestling in the box was a large and very lovely cake, an expensive, cream-covered confection whose surface and sides were densely decorated with scalloped petals of dark chocolate, with little bursts of dark cherry juice bruising the cream.

'Shall we have some?' ventured Lucy.

'It's your sister's. Won't she mind?'

A brief silence followed, in which two thoughts occurred to them – yes, Anthea would mind, but hey, who cared anyway?

Lucy rummaged for a suitable knife, saying, 'She never gets back till after seven. We'll have gone by then. I bet she won't miss a couple of slices. I mean, come on, she can't eat an entire cake all on her own.' She dug into the rich cake, slicing through the velvety petals of chocolate and into the cherry-juice-soaked sponge. 'Here, grab a couple of plates.' Lucy cut two generous slabs of expensive patisserie gateau and lifted them out of the box and on to plates. She licked her thumb and glanced at the unopened chilled bottle of Blue Label Smirnoff. The luscious plundering of the cake had bred recklessness in her, and besides, breaching the virgin cake and cracking open the pristine vodka at the same time had a fitting coherence. 'Let's have some of this, too.'

'You're joking, right?'

'Oh, she won't notice. She's always got a bottle open. Here.' Lucy took two tumblers from the cupboard and splashed a couple of inches of vodka into each. 'Come on, let's go and see what's on MTV.'

They took their spoils through to the living room, where they watched music videos, bitched and gossiped, ate cake and drank vodka for the next half hour. Then, on the basis that the cake had been started and that Anthea wouldn't miss a tiny bit more, they had another slice each. At half five they were rolling around on Anthea's sofa, joking and laughing and happily tipsy, when they heard the front door open.

Lucy froze. 'It's Ant! What's she doing back? She never gets home this early! Oh my God! I am *so* dead! Quick!' She grabbed the plates and the vodka glasses and hurried to the kitchen. Just as she was returning, Anthea came into the living room and gave Lucy and Georgia a baleful look.

'We're back to this, are we? I'd hoped you'd given up coming round and marauding my flat, Lucy. And who said you could bring your friends round? I'm fed up with this.' She pulled off her jacket and chucked it with her bag on to a chair. She headed for the kitchen, untying her blonde hair. 'I'll bet you've been at my drink again.'

Georgia gazed after her, feeling a mixture of admiring awe at Anthea's careless, gazelle-like beauty as she sauntered to the kitchen, and an incipient sense of guilty horror at the thought of the despoiled cake. Lucy and Georgia exchanged glances.

Anthea's voice came screeching from the kitchen. 'Lucy, you prize little cow! What have you done to my cake?' She raged back into the room, blonde hair flying loose, eyes blazing. 'I could bloody murder you! I picked that up especially from Patisserie Valerie at lunchtime! It was for Chantal's birthday tonight! My God, how could the pair of you *do* that? This is the absolute bloody limit, Lucy! This is the last, last time you set foot in my flat – ever! Give me my key now!' She held out her hand. 'Come on!' Sulkily Lucy dug in her coat pocket for the key and flung it at Anthea, who went on, 'You are such an immature little bitch – d'you know that, Lucy? When are you going to grow up and stop your pathetic behaviour? My God, you're nearly eighteen, but how can anyone take you seriously when you behave like this? You're like a spoiled thirteen-year-old!'

'That's not what Leo thinks,' retorted Lucy. She was angry, humiliated, and a little drunk. Georgia huddled nervously on the sofa, not sure whether she was enjoying the developing row or not.

'Oh, you *are* joking, aren't you?' laughed Anthea. 'The way you come on to him – my God! It's a total embarrassment! If you have to get a crush on someone, choose someone your own age. We both feel sorry for you.'

'Really? Then how come he slept with me while you were in Bermuda?'

Anthea laughed again, but with less certainty. 'Please, keep your adolescent fantasising to yourself! Leo wouldn't look at you.'

'He's done a lot more than that. D'you want to know what happened? We spent Saturday night at his place, in his bed. He told me he'd always wanted to go to bed with a seventeen year-old.'

Anthea's face was stricken with disbelief. 'You little bitch! What is it with you and your lies?'

'It's not lies! Your lovely Leo's been coming on to me ever since we first met here, in your flat, only you were too up your own arse to notice! He likes young girls, the younger the better – he told me. He told me it while he was making love to me – '

Anthea fetched her sister a hefty slap across the face, so hard that it sent Lucy stumbling backwards into a chair. Georgia looked on in thrilled horror. 'Don't you dare, Lucy!' hissed Anthea. 'I'm warning you!'

Lucy put her hand to the red mark glowing on her cheek, and smiled shakily. 'You just can't stand to hear the truth, can you? Well, ask him! Ask him if I didn't spend the night with him! Then we'll see who's lying. I was there all Saturday night, in his house, in his bed, and in the morning he drove me home. I told Mum I was at Georgia's.' She turned to Georgia. 'Georgia knew what was going on. Didn't you?'

Georgia nodded weakly.

'You're lying, I know you are!' But Anthea was now far from certain. Lucy could see it in her eyes.

'He made love to me, Anthea! It happened! Why would I make it up?'

'God, why do you ever do anything?' She reached down and grabbed Lucy by her shoulders, dragging her to her feet. 'Tell me – look me in the eyes and tell me you're not lying, you little cow!'

'I'm not! Your precious Leo took me to bed! You want proof? I even know what kind of sheets and pillowcases he has – blue ones, with little white squares round the edges. Now do you believe me? How would I know that if I hadn't been in his bed?'

'Why?' There were angry tears in Anthea's eyes. 'Why would you do something like that, Lucy?'

'I did it because I wanted to, and so did he! Deal with it!' Lucy grabbed her shoes and put them on, picked up her belongings and stormed out, with Georgia not far behind her.

As they went downstairs, Georgia gasped, 'My God, Luce! That was such a total lie! You told me you that when you got back to his place you decided you didn't fancy him after all, and that nothing happened!'

'Yeah, well – she deserves it, telling me off like I'm a kid. I mean, how humiliating was that? God, she's so up herself! Let her believe it. I don't care.'

28

Oblivious of all that was happening in Fulham, Leo spent the evening with Michael and Anthony, discussing events in chambers. They agreed that a chambers' meeting should be held to consider the entire matter, but Leo decided he would speak personally to Maurice beforehand. The next day he went to see him, taking with him the copy of Melanie's reference.

'I take it you know by now that it was Roger who downloaded the documents from your computer and sent them round the building?' said Leo. 'It was an inexcusable thing to do, of course, and he'll be making an apology to you. However, it seems he was concerned about this.' Leo laid the piece of paper on Maurice's desk.

Maurice didn't even glance at it. 'I don't care what concerns he had, he had no business – '

'Well, hold on,' interrupted Leo. 'There's more to this issue than Roger's invasion of your privacy, unwarranted though it was. We can't just ignore what he turned up. This reference, for a start.'

Maurice picked up the paper, and his face grew uneasy. 'This is privileged.'

'No, it isn't. You're a lawyer. You know you can't write whatever you like about someone – not if a prospective employer is going to read it. It can be construed as defamation. And why the hell would you want to say any of this about Melanie? She was excellent, as you well know.' Maurice shrugged, evidently discomfited. 'Now, I suggest you withdraw this, and write something halfway decent, or I will. You're jeopardising her employment chances.'

'I can amend it, I suppose.'

'Do that. I want to see it when it's done. Now – ' Leo sat down. ' – we come to the more important matter of the fee notes which Roger disclosed. I wanted to speak to you about these first, in case it might save you unnecessary embarrassment at the chamber's meeting. It appears on the face of it that you've been billing clients direct. I wondered if you had anything to say about it?'

'I've done nothing improper, if that's what you mean. Some of it relates to offshore work which came through an acquaintance of mine – a lawyer, admittedly, but since solicitors weren't involved there was no referral aspect – '

'You know that doesn't matter. All work which comes to you should go through the system.'

' – and the vast majority relate to work done for an Italian company, in which I happen to be a forty per cent shareholder. Those invoices were merely raised for accounting purposes, and to identify the work done. My payment comes in the form of share options.'

'I take it you've been spending a good deal of time doing work for this Italian company?'

'You could say that.'

'Which I suppose would account for your billing figures being down. The company's called Perinetti, isn't it?'

'Correct.'

'And your wife's maiden name, as I recall, is Perini.'

'What a lot you know.'

'The point is, Maurice, there are some members of chambers who would say – and I might put myself among them – that since you've been using chambers' facilities to spend your time doing work for a family company, you should pay for the privilege. You've been avoiding paying your fair whack. You know perfectly well that all work has to go through the clerks. I have to tell you they're not very happy.'

'When are they ever?'

'You're pocketing their commission. You're by-passing the system. Added to which, behaviour like this could get us into trouble with the Bar Council and the Inland Revenue. Not something the other members of chambers will be too pleased about.'

'It's nothing to do with them. This is private work, so it's a private matter.'

'Not if it raises problems for chambers.'

Maurice threw Leo a cynical look. 'You see this as an ideal opportunity to stir up resentment against me, don't you? I still maintain I've done nothing wrong.'

Leo rose. 'That's for the meeting to decide. I'm calling it for five o'clock tomorrow. You can put your side of things then.'

Leo left Maurice's room without another word.

29

Leo had arranged with Rachel that he would pick Oliver up from school on Wednesday afternoon. He worked through lunchtime to make sure he could leave at three, giving him forty minutes to reach Chiswick, which he assumed would be ample time mid-afternoon. He was unprepared, however, for the swarms of traffic produced by the daily school run, and it took him longer than he had anticipated to negotiate the Land Rovers and double-parked people carriers which choked the side roads near to Oliver's school.

By the time he had managed to park the car and get to the school, it was almost four, and Oliver was inside, waiting with the teacher on duty. Leo apologised for being late, gave Oliver a hug, and was just about to leave with him when the deputy headmistress, whom he recognised from Oliver's first day, came out of her office, waving an envelope.

'Mr Davies, a gentleman left this for Mrs Davies earlier today. I was going to give it to her first thing tomorrow morning, but since you're here, perhaps you can give it to her.'

Leo took the envelope. 'A gentleman? What did he look like?'

'Well, let's see. He was a very tall man, foreign I'd say, with dark hair, and what you'd call designer stubble.' She enunciated these last words with delicate irony, intending to convey to Leo that he hadn't really been what she would classify as a 'gentleman' at all.

'Right,' said Leo. 'Thank you.'

He hurried Oliver to the car, then got in and opened the envelope. It was an unpleasant letter, conveying non-specific threats aimed at both Rachel and Oliver. Had Rachel read it, she would have been frightened and distressed, but she would have had no way of connecting it to Leo or his work. Nor would the police. It was, Leo realised, a warning intended directly for him, from the man who had come to see him.

Leo swore under his breath. So much for protecting his position in relation to the Proceeds of Crime Act. This was what came of indicating to Sir Dudley that he knew what was going on. He'd just made things worse.

'Daddy, you said the S word,' said Oliver reprovingly.

'Sorry,' said Leo. 'That was bad. Come on, let's get you home and give you some tea. Then we can play, and I'll take you back to Mummy's before bedtime.'

He stuffed the letter, which he had no intention of disclosing to Rachel, into his coat pocket, thanking providence that if was he, and not the child-minder, who'd picked Oliver up today.

Pride, and the suspicion that Lucy might have been telling the truth, prevented Anthea from confronting Leo. Instead she took her unhappiness off to Lola, who, from her elegant penthouse overlooking the river, offered the usual comforts of champagne and a little coke.

'I couldn't very well turn up at Chantal's' party without the cake, so I had to go hunting round for another.'

'Did you find one?' asked Lolly, deftly cutting thin, snowy lines of cocaine on the small glass plate in front of her. Just enough for a little evening 'sniffter', as she called it. She was very fond of that joke.

'Eventually, in a patisserie in Pimlico, but it wasn't spectacular. I'd ordered the other one specially. And those moronic teenagers ate half of it! I could absolutely have killed them both.'

'What happened to the other half?' asked Lolly wistfully. 'Did you eat it?'

'Darling, as if I would, with you in the world.' She delved into a carrier bag and brought out the cake box.

'How fab. We'll have it in a minute. Here – you do that, while I get us some shampers.'

She proffered the little mirror to Anthea, who snorted her couple of lines as daintily as it was possible to do, then shook back her blonde hair and sighed. 'I don't usually do this stuff, you know. But right now I need it. I still haven't told you the worst bit.' Her eyes filled with tears. 'Oh, Lolly!' she wailed.

'What?' asked Lola in alarm, setting down the glasses and the bottle. She put her arms round her friend and let her weep for a little while, before disengaging herself to pop the champagne and pour it out. 'Here, get this down you – ' She handed Anthea a glass. ' – and tell me what's wrong.'

Anthea dabbed her tears. 'That little cow of a sister of mine tells me she slept with Leo while I was away.'

'Oh, crap!'

'What?' Anthea eyed her friend doubtfully. 'You mean – crap, as in rubbish, or crap, as in, oh no?'

'The first. He wouldn't do something like that.'

'He might. She would.'

'Would she?'

Anthea knocked back her champagne and gave a miserable, impatient sniff. 'She's had a crush on him for a while. She's always finding excuses to be there when he comes round.'

'So what? That tells you nothing. Oh for God's sake, Leo wouldn't sleep with your sister! She's only seventeen.'

'She said he said he liked younger girls. And look at her, Lolly – she can be quite the sex kitten when she wants to. Bitch,' she murmured, and took another swig of champagne. 'I seriously believe it might have happened, Lolly. Her putrid friend Georgia backed her up.'

'Like she would know.'

'She seemed to. If it happened, she was in on it somehow. My God, Lucy even described his bloody bed linen to me! How could she do that if she wasn't there?' Anthea put her face in her hands.

There was a brief silence as Lola considered the possibilities. 'Don't you trust him?' she asked at length.

'Oh my God, Lolly!' wailed Anthea. 'What are you *talking* about? Of course I don't trust him!' She beat her fists against the sofa cushions in frustration. 'I don't want him to be that kind of man – it's so boring! I just don't want him sleeping with my little sister! *Half*-sister,' she added. 'Her father's to blame for how awful she is.'

'What makes you think she's really slept with him? She's probably just winding you up because you were upset about the cake. Shall we have some, by the way?'

'Lolly, she said she stayed at his house on Saturday night. She said he made love to her and drove her home the next morning. Now, either he did – or he didn't.'

Lola shrugged. 'You may not trust him, but the least you can do is ask him. Shall we have that cake now?'

Anthea threw herself back against the cushions and groaned. 'How abject is that going to sound? I mean, imagine *asking* him if he slept with Lucy! My God...'

'Well, you don't have to be that direct.' Lola tenderly lifted the lid of the cake box. 'Say she told you some stuff about staying over at his house, and take it from there.'

'I could, I suppose.' She blew her nose and looked at Lola. 'He wouldn't, would he? I mean, what kind of man would sleep with their girlfriend's teenage sister?'

Lola decided it was best to leave this unanswered. 'I'll get a knife for the cake,' she said.

When they had finished cake, coke and champagne, Lola said, 'I'm sorry you can't stay longer, sweetie, but I have to go out in fifteen minutes.'

'That's OK, Lolly,' said Anthea, putting on her shoes. 'I'm going to go home and have a bath. And work out what to do.'

'You've probably got nothing to worry about. You know what teenage girls are like – it's probably all in her mind.'

'Well, if I find out it's not, I'm not sure who I'll kill first – her or him.'

When she got home Anthea decided there was no way that she was going to ring Leo. The idea of calling him and demanding to know whether he'd slept with Lucy was too debasing. She ran a bath and lay in it, soaking and thinking. If anything had happened between Leo and Lucy, that was the end. What she'd said to Lola was true – there was a certain piquancy to the knowledge that Leo might not be the most trustworthy lover in the world, but there were limits. But why would he do such a thing? She'd really thought Leo was beginning to value what they had together, that their mutual pretence at its inconsequentiality masked something deeper. Maybe she was kidding herself. A sick, cold feeling of certainty began to take hold of her. Of course it was true. How could it not be? Lucy wouldn't know what kind of sheets he had on his bed if she hadn't slept in them. She wouldn't make up a story like that without some evidence to back it up. An image of Leo and Lucy together presented itself; Anthea gave a little whimper and sank down beneath the water to obliterate it. After a few seconds of immersion she thought she heard the phone. She emerged with a gasp and splutter, and listened. Definitely the phone.

With a sigh she launched her lovely body out of the bath, pulled on a towelling robe, and padded to her room, wringing her wet hair with her hands. She lifted the receiver. 'Hello?'

'Anthea, it's Leo.' Her heart gave a little dip. 'I'm still in chambers. Not the best of days. I thought I'd ring and see if you'd like some company later this evening.'

Anthea sat down on the bed. The sound of his voice brought it all together for her – so cool and arrogant, full of the easy assumption that he'd got away with it. You snake, Leo, she thought. Coming on like you can do that to me and I won't find out. Her voice was cold as she replied, 'I don't think so.'

''No? Why's that? You sound fed up.'

'I imagine you'd probably prefer something younger. Something in the sixteen, seventeen year-old range, perhaps?'

There was a pause, then Leo suddenly realised where this was coming from. He sighed and said, 'What has Lucy been saying?' And as soon as the words were uttered, he wished them back.

'My God, I didn't think you'd admit it that easily,' said Anthea, trying to keep her voice steady. 'But then, why wouldn't you? You can hardly deny it, not in the circumstances. Not now that she's told me all about it.'

'Anthea, whatever she's told you isn't true, I assure you.' Why in God's name, he asked himself, hadn't he had the sense to tell Anthea exactly what had happened that night? Because tiresome and silly as Lucy was, he had never believed she would be this malevolent.

'Leo, do you think I'm stupid? If it was all lies, you wouldn't have a clue what I was talking about! But obviously you know all too well! You slept with my sister while I was away! She stayed in your house, in your bed!'

'Anthea, it wasn't like that. If you'll stop yelling and let me explain – '

'Oh? What was it like, then? Do you deny she stayed there?'

'No, but – '

'And that you slept with her?'

'No — I mean, yes! Yes, I deny it! She was at a night club, and I went to pick her up – '

'And brought her home and fucked her! Admit it, why don't you? She has!'

'She's lying. She's lying because – because she wants to hurt you. Or me. I don't know.' The pause at the other end made Leo hope she was listening, and perhaps growing calmer. But Anthea was merely trying to muffle her sobs.

'Leo, you took her to bed! I know you did!' She clenched her teeth, tearful and enraged. 'Don't you dare try to deny it!'

'I didn't – '

'Do you? Do you deny it? Do you deny she was in your bed?'

'No, but that was the next morning, when she – '

Anthea let out a screech of anger. 'My God, you're such a weasel! Trying to talk around this like there are excuses to be made! You – picked – up – my – seventeen – year – old – sister –' She beat her fist on the bed with each word, ' – and – slept – with – her – while – I – was – AWAY!'

'If you would just stop screeching and let me explain – '

146

'Don't you tell me I'm screeching! I am not screeching!'

'Yes, you are. Calm down, and let me – '

'No, I don't want to hear any more from you!' She took a couple of deep breaths. 'You've said enough. She was there, with you, in your bed – all of it, you've admitted. You are a piece of slime, Leo, and I never want to see you again.' She switched off the phone and flung it, then herself, on the bed and wept.

Leo listened to the buzz of the line, then hung up. Why was it, he wondered, that after half a lifetime spent honing his powers of rhetoric, he had handled that so spectacularly badly? Perhaps because Anthea had unwittingly followed the golden rule of cross-examination by asking only questions to which she knew the answers – or thought she knew the answers. But this was the heart of the problem – whatever spiteful lies Lucy had told, a good deal of the damning circumstantial evidence happened to be true. Hence his wretched performance in trying to set the matter straight. Perhaps he should have lied outright, and said the entire thing was a fabrication, instead of admitting to bits of it. That wouldn't have helped, though, because, like a fool, he had indicated from the outset that he knew she was talking about Lucy.

Leo leaned back in his chair and groaned. Then he picked up the phone and dialled Anthea's number again. She answered after a couple of rings and told him to go to hell. Not tearfully, not emotionally – but coldly and dispassionately. Not a good sign. So what was he to do? Even if he were to find a way of getting her to listen to him, the true story was never going to sound particularly convincing. It would be his word against Lucy's, and since Anthea already believed whatever lurid version of events Lucy had chosen to give, he didn't stand much of a chance.

Time for a little word with Lucy.

30

Leo waited outside Lucy's school the following afternoon, feeling less like a predatory paedophile than he had expected. There were plenty of other lone adults sitting idly in their expensive cars near the school gates, leafing through magazines or talking on their mobiles, though most of them were mothers. It had, of course, occurred to Leo that his mission could well prove entirely fruitless; Lucy might have some after-school activity; she might have gone home at lunchtime; she might not even be in school that day. Still, it was the only way he knew of getting hold of her to speak to her. Her lies to Anthea had created a situation which would not be healed or resolved by the passage of time. Only Lucy could set this right, and Leo was determined to make this clear to her.

Four o'clock came and went. Streams of chattering pupils spilled out of the school gates. He scanned the faces of the older girls, but no Lucy. Then, just as he was about to give up, he saw her dawdling towards the school coach with another girl, whom he recognised as Georgia, her friend from the Soho night-club.

Leo put the car in gear and slipped out of his parking space. The waiting cars had cleared somewhat, and he was able to pull up next to Lucy as she strolled along the pavement. She glanced towards the car just as he slid the electric window down, and stopped when she saw him.

The sight of Leo waiting outside her school gates provoked two responses in Lucy – one of childlike guilt and fear, and the other a weird sense of pleasure that she had created a situation where Leo had to come looking for her. She felt in control, like all the cards were in her hand.

Leo leaned over, the engine still running. 'Lucy?'

Her pretty face assumed a haughty, impertinent expression. 'Yes?'

'I'd like to talk to you.' He leaned across and opened the passenger door. Lucy hesitated for a moment on the pavement. She glanced at Georgia, then got into Leo's car, mouthing 'Catch you later' at her friend. She chucked her school bag on to the rear seat and flicked back her dark hair, looking mildly apprehensive but generally pleased with herself.

There was silence for a moment. Leo sat letting the engine run, tapping the wheel with his fingers.

Lucy gave him a challenging look. She didn't like his silence. 'What?'

'Come on,' said Leo, suddenly putting the car into gear and moving away from the pavement. They drove slowly through the busy streets.

'Where are we going?' asked Lucy.

'I'm taking you home,' said Leo.

'How d'you mean?' She wondered, for a small, thrilling moment, whether he had changed his mind about the other night, and whether they were going to drive to his place in Chelsea and make wild, passionate love in the bed he had kicked her out of not so long ago.

'How do I mean?' replied Leo. 'I mean home – your home. Where you live with your mother.'

'Why? What's going on?'

'You know what's going on. The lies you told your sister have caused a lot of unhappiness and trouble. You have from now till we get to Kensington to agree to tell her the truth and set matters straight, or –'

'Or what? You don't tell me what to do. Like I care about you and her.'

'Or I speak to your mother, tell her exactly what's been happening.'

Lucy gave a gasp of disbelief. 'Seriously? You seriously think involving my mother is going to help you?' She laughed. 'My God, Leo, you are so screwed! All I have to do is tell her my version, only I'll make it even worse, say that I didn't want to but you made me, gave me loads to drink and stuff, and say that you're telling lies because things have got mucked up with you and Anthea, and she'll – '

Leo brought the car to a sudden halt at the side of the road. 'Lucy!' he snapped. 'Shut up!' Lucy's expression as he looked at her was one of truculent defiance, but he could see apprehension in her eyes. 'Your mother is a grown-up. I am a grown-up. When grown-ups talk intelligently to one another, things happen that children don't understand. You are a child, and a very nasty, spoilt one. However much your mother loves you, I'm sure she's under no illusions as to the kind of child you are. So she'll believe me. I can assure you – she will believe me, and she won't give an ounce of credit to any lies you tell. I happen to be very fond of your sister, and I refuse to allow a nasty kid like you to wreck things. And if you insist on carrying on with your lies, I shall involve Georgia. She has nothing to gain by supporting you in this sordid little sham of yours, and a great deal to lose. Oh, and on the grown-up point, I may even speak to your school.' He could see the fear and anger burning in her eyes. 'It gets worse and worse, doesn't it?'

'You wouldn't!' She stared at him with a sullen, challenging gaze, then suddenly it softened to one of unhappy supplication. She reached out and touched his hand as it rested on the steering wheel, and moved closer to him. 'Leo, I only did it because you hurt me. You didn't want me. I felt really upset. And then Anthea had a go at me, and I just said it to spite both of you. But it's not too late. If you still want me – ' Her soft, young mouth was very close to his, babbling her adolescent confusion, and he was sorely tempted to kiss the idiocy right out of her. Just in time he drew away, moving her hand from his thigh, where it had slipped.

'OK. That's enough. Stop. I'm not buying this little act either.' He put the car in gear and pulled away from the kerb. 'Come on, let's go home and have a word with your mother.'

Lucy scowled at him. 'I hate you. I really, really hate you, Leo.'

'Yes, that sounds more like it. Honesty at last. Now, are you going to speak to Anthea and tell her what really happened? To spare your pride, you can keep in the bit about you getting drunk and incapable. I won't tell her you tried to set me up.'

'You really think I'm just going to do what you say? How do you know I won't make it even worse? How do you know I won't tell her you got me in your car and threatened me?'

They had reached the end of Lucy's street. Leo stopped the car. He let a silence elapse, and when he spoke his tone was as reasonable as he could make it. 'Because, Lucy, I don't think you hate your sister that much. I think you love her. How do you think she feels, believing what you told her? How do you think it makes you look to her? She is so fond of you, and if you let this lie go on, she will never look at you in the same way again. Right now she doesn't just believe I've deceived and hurt her – she believes you have, too. I don't think you want to see her so unhappy, or to make this rotten mess of yours even worse than it is.' Lucy's young eyes suddenly brightened with miserable, genuine tears, and Leo knew he had his moment. 'Look, I know it's not going to be the easiest or the pleasantest thing to tell her the truth, but it's the only way to put things right.'

He watched her face, watched the conflicting emotions that crossed it as she struggled to salvage her pride.

'OK,' she said at last. She sniffed, trying to blink back her tears, and Leo reached into the glove compartment and pulled out a tissue and handed it to her. She dabbed at smudges of mascara and muttered, 'I'm not spoilt and nasty, you know. That stuff you said.'

'Good. I didn't think you were. Just go and sort it out.'

She turned round and hauled her bag from the back seat and on to her lap, and sat there for a miserable moment. She looked about twelve, lovely and troubled. Poor Oliver, thought Leo – he had no idea what was coming in a few years' time.

Without another word she got out of the car and set off towards her house. He watched her walk up to the front door and take out her key. She let herself in, the front door closed, and

Leo slid down in his seat with a shuddering sigh. He had to admit now that he had taken an extraordinary risk. She could have done exactly as she had threatened – she might have lied to her mother, even to her school, if it had gone that far, and got away with it. Children did these days. She was a precocious little minx with vicious capabilities and mixed-up emotions, and he had just gambled his professional career on her. Still, he hadn't spent twenty five years turning himself into an expert judge of character for nothing. The idly manipulative, self-centred brat was essentially a somewhat confused but innately decent teenager. And lethally sexy, more than even she knew. Definitely worth re-visiting in ten years time, by which time, unfortunately, she wouldn't look at him twice.

He sat there, reflecting for a moment. Then he pulled out his mobile phone and sent a text to Anthea. **'I think your little sister has something to tell you.'** Poor Lucy. That was going to be a difficult confession to have to make. He thought about what she'd said – how she could make it even worse for him by telling Anthea that he'd picked her up from school and threatened her. No, she probably wouldn't do that. On the whole, he thought she'd had enough of lying. He could see it in her eyes, the way he'd seen it in the eyes of dozens of witnesses. After a while, when lying got complex and exhausting, most of them just wanted to give up and tell the truth.

Still, he wouldn't rest easy until he knew that Lucy had spoken to Anthea and set matters straight, and who knew how long that would take?

31

As he sat talking and smoking with the other men, Marko watched Viktor, waiting to see if he was going to go to Irina's room. Viktor had taken to visiting her every day now, something he had never done with any of the other girls. It wasn't just that Marko was jealous – he hated the way he would find Irina weeping an hour, two hours after Viktor had been with her. He shouldn't care. Viktor was the boss, he could do what he wanted with the girls. But Marko had a thing about Irina. He liked her. He liked the way she teased him when they played cards, made him feel like a boy. Like a kind of stupid boy. He didn't want her thinking him stupid. For a few days now he'd been planning something he could do to make her look at him differently.

Viktor stood around bantering for a while, then announced he was going out and would be back later that evening.

'Hey, Marko!' he snapped. 'Get out there! Someone should be watching the rooms.'

Marko went out to the corridor. He waited till Viktor had disappeared, then went to Irina's door and rapped softly. She was on her own, lying on the bed, her face blank, staring at the ceiling. Her eyes moved towards Marko, then away.

'I don't feel like cards, Marko.'

Marko came and sat down in the chair near her bed. 'I haven't come to play cards. I've come to talk.'

She gave him a longer glance. 'What about?'

Marko hesitated, rubbing his bristly chin with one hand, then said softly, 'I want to do something for you.'

She studied his face. He was like a big, stupid dog. She'd known for a while now that Marko had a crush on her. You could always tell. It was a body language thing – the way he sat, the way he kept his eyes fixed on her face for too long when they were playing cards.

'What kind of thing?'

He wasn't good with words. It took him ten halting minutes to tell Irina how he felt about her, how he had this idea that, if she felt the same way, he could get her out of here and they could go somewhere together. Irina listened in silence. She felt absolutely nothing for Marko. She didn't think she'd ever feel anything for any man again. She wasn't grateful to him for playing cards with her, or being halfway decent to her, because to feel any of that would be to legitimise all of this shit. But she was prepared to use him. She would use him any way she could to get out of here.

'I don't know if you have feelings for me,' he said, casting his eyes down. 'I think you might.'

Irina sat up and put a hand on his. He so much wanted to believe her that it didn't take a lot of words to convince him she felt the same. To make sure, she leaned forward and kissed his flabby mouth. It was horrible, but the thought of what she stood to gain kindled such genuine excitement in her that she was able to kiss him as though she meant it.

'It's gonna be easy,' said Marko. 'I'm the one guarding you – I'm the one to get you out of here.' Already he felt capable, in control, someone she could look up to. 'It's a big risk for me. After he finds out what's happened he's gonna want to kill me. You know that?'

Irina knew, and she couldn't care less. If Marko finished up with his tiny brain blown out of the side of his big, fat head, it was his look-out. That, presumably, was one of the risks you took when you made the lifestyle choice of working for Viktor Kroitor. She felt neither pity or gratefulness. She smiled her sweetest smile, and the hope in her heart allowed her eyes to fill with real tears. Let him think they were for him, stupid man. 'Thank you, Marko. You are doing all this for me – I can't believe it.' She kissed him again.

They talked it through and decided it was just a question of taking the best available opportunity to leave the hotel. Marko reckoned any evening – tonight, or tomorrow night, or the one after that – when things were busier and men were coming and going from the girls' rooms. After all, Marko and the other guys were the only thing that stood between the girls and the outside world. He was more worried about the immediate aftermath, and going somewhere Viktor wouldn't find them.

'How much money have you got?' Irina asked him.

'About two hundred pounds. Not enough.'

'What about Viktor? How much cash does he carry?'

Marko shrugged. 'A lot. I've seen him with wads of cash. He's like that. But what d'you think I'm gonna do – rob him? I'm not that stupid, Irina.'

'You don't have to,' she said. 'I will. Next time he comes to see me. He always puts his jacket over the chair beforehand. All you do is call him away – make something up, I don't know. Give me enough time to go through his pockets.'

Marko nodded slowly. 'That's good.'

'But it means we have to go straight afterwards, before he finds out.'

Marko nodded again. 'That's a big risk.'

'Exactly. And it's my risk, not yours, if you think about it. So you've got to be really clever, and really careful. OK?'

'For sure,' replied Marko, gazing soulfully at her.

Viktor came back at six with a couple of friends, and after chatting a while with the other men, went to Irina's room. Marko watched him go. How long had she said? Seven minutes. Long enough for him to get his jacket off, but not so long that he'd already started. Irina had told him that the things Viktor liked to do to her got worse each time. He tried not to think of this as he glanced at his watch. After this, Viktor would never have the chance to do anything to her ever again. Already Marko was beginning to feel like a protector, a hero, and he liked this new idea of himself. It was better than what he was now – a small-time gangster who got paid to hang around hotels keeping an eye on things, driving cars, hurting people when necessary.

He'd only got into because he was big and tough, and because the money had been better than anything else he could make. But it was shit work, dirty work. It was pretty boring, too. With Irina, he would get into something better, make more money for both of them. She was smart and beautiful, Irina – with her, he could do anything.

He was so busy day-dreaming that he almost forgot what he was meant to be doing. Shit – Viktor must have been in there nearly ten minutes. Marko jumped to his feet and went out into the corridor to Irina's room. He rapped on the door.

There was silence for a moment, then Viktor's voice shouted 'What?'

'It's Marko, boss. I need a word.'

Viktor came to the door in his shirt-sleeves, not best pleased. 'Yeah, what?'

Marko had already worked out what he would say. 'That guy's downstairs. The one we sold the dope to yesterday. He says it's no good. He wants to see you.'

'No way.'

'He's really mad, talking about sending some of his boys over. I think you should see him.'

Viktor swore under his breath. 'I'll go down.' He came out, closing the door behind him. Marko watched him go to the lift, wondering what he was meant to do next.

Irina sat on the bed, staring at Viktor's jacket. Should she? The idea was suddenly terrifying. What if he came back in and caught her? Had he gone downstairs or not? Why didn't Marko tell her? God, Marko was stupid. Stupid, stupid, stupid. She got up and went to the door, putting her ear to it. She couldn't hear voices. She went back to the chair and stared again at the jacket. Then, heart thumping, she slipped her hand into the inside pocket and it closed round a fat wallet. Yes! She pulled it out and flipped it open, and saw it was stuffed with notes. She had no idea what their value was, but they had the look of decent money. Credit cards too. She was about to move away from the chair, when the door opened. Terror tightened her throat. She turned, and it was Marko.

'My God, you frightened me!'

'Come on!' Marko's own eyes were wide and anxious. 'Come on! There's no one about. But move! He'll come back up when he finds there's no one there!'

Irina grabbed her jacket from the wardrobe, and picked up her bag and stuffed Viktor's wallet into it. Her hands were shaking so badly it made everything slow. Swearing, almost sobbing with fear, certain Viktor would be back in the room before she could even get out of it, she tugged the zip shut.

'Come on!' Marko's voice was urgent, almost frantic. They both knew, in this moment, how bad it would be for them if things went wrong. She hurried to the door, and Marko took her hand, and the next thing they were heading along the corridor towards the staircase. If Viktor came out of the lift in the next ten seconds and found her gone, they wouldn't even make it as far as the street. The stairwell seemed to go on forever, but at last they were at the bottom, and there was the door leading to the lobby.

'What if he's still out there?' said Irina.

'I'll look,' said Marko. 'Hold on.'

She let him go, counting the seconds. They seemed endless. And then he was back. 'Come on. He's gone up.'

That Viktor had gone back up meant that they had very little time to get out and away. But as she walked as calmly as possible across the lobby, past the reception desk, she could see and smell the air of the street beyond, and taste her freedom.

Then they were outside, and Marko was just about dragging her towards a taxi passing with its light on. They got in, and Marko told the driver to go to Euston Station.

'Why did you say that place?' asked Irina.

Marko shrugged, his eyes still combing the street anxiously. 'I don't know. It's a big station with trains that go to other cities.'

She realised he had no kind of a plan, but it didn't matter anyway. She was going to be rid of him soon enough.

When they reached the station they went into a Starbucks, bought coffees and sat down. Irina took Viktor's wallet from her bag and began to go through its contents. She pulled out the thick bundle of notes and showed it to Marko.

'How much is this?' she asked.

Marko stared at his boss's money with frightened eyes. A sheaf of fifties, and the rest twenties. 'A lot.' Then he added, 'Put it away.'

Irina stuffed the notes back in the wallet. She looked to see what else was in it. Receipts, credit cards... She pulled out a piece of paper and unfolded it. She read Leo's name and address. 'What's this?' she asked, showing it to Marko.

Marko took the piece of paper. 'Some guy. A lawyer. Viktor paid him a visit to make sure he kept quiet about some business or other. I drove him round there.' He nodded. 'Nice house. Expensive.'

'He's not a friend of Viktor's?'

'No way.' Marko watched as Irina folded the paper up and put it back in the wallet. Suddenly Marko's mobile phone began to buzz. He pulled it from his pocket and stared at the screen with anxious eyes. 'Shit. It's Viktor.'

'Don't answer it!'

'You think I'm mad?' He put the phone on the table, where it buzzed a few more times before falling silent. Marko rubbed his hands over his big face, trying to think. How long till Viktor put it all together? Maybe he already had. 'Listen,' said Marko, 'we need to get out of London fast. We need to go right away, to some other city. I'm gonna see what trains there are and buy us tickets. OK?'

'OK.' Irina nodded.

She watched him cross the concourse, then disappear into the milling streams of people. Irina put Viktor's wallet in her bag and got up. As she was about to leave, she saw Marko's mobile still lying on the table. She picked it up and thrust it into her bag. She left the coffee shop, glanced once in the direction in which Marko had gone, then turned and headed quickly the other way towards the exit. In a few seconds she was out on the street and, without knowing where she was or where she was going, she turned right and started walking.

Just keep walking, she thought, and he'll never find you. But as the seconds passed she became convinced Marko had come out of the station looking for her, that he was behind her and would catch up with her any minute. She had to get away further and faster.

She saw a black cab with its light on, like the one she and Marko had taken from the hotel, and waved her hand. It pulled over, and she got in.

'Where to, love?' asked the cabbie. She met his eye in the mirror. Her heart was beating painfully hard. Where was she to go? She knew no one in this city. She had no passport, no papers, nothing. She didn't want to be arrested. She just wanted to get home, but she didn't know how to do that. She needed someone to help her. She dived into her bag and pulled out Viktor's wallet, and from it she took the piece of paper and unfolded it. She stared at it for a moment. A lawyer. From what Marko had said, this man was not Viktor's friend. That didn't necessarily make him *her* friend, but it was a name and an address, and it was worth trying. What had she to lose? There was nowhere else to go.

She handed the paper to the cabbie and said, 'Please. This place.'

The cabbie set his meter running and drove off through the traffic in the direction of Chelsea.

32

That evening, when he heard the doorbell ring, Leo took the precaution of looking through the little spyhole in the front door, something he had never bothered to do in the past, to make sure it wasn't another Ukrainian gangster in a dodgy coat. What he saw on his doorstep was a worried-looking, dark-haired young woman, apparently on her own.

Leo opened the door. The girl looked at him, saying nothing, her expression still anxious.

'Can I help you?' asked Leo.

Irina had no idea what she was getting into here. Anyone that Viktor knew, even an enemy of his, could be just as bad as he was. She stared at Leo. He was a handsome man, with silver hair and blue eyes, and a face that looked kind – but kind looks could mean nothing.

'I need help,' she ventured. Her voice was hesitant, her accent very thick. Not another Eastern European, thought Leo wearily. They were everywhere these days. What did this one want? Was she collecting for something, or begging? She didn't look like a beggar – her clothes were cheaply fashionable, and she herself was very attractive.

'Look,' said Leo, digging in his pocket, 'this isn't something I usually do, but take this. Go on – off you go.' He held out a twenty pound note.

Irina looked at it, then at him. He had spoken so quickly she hadn't understood anything he'd said. She shook her head. 'No. Not money.' Leo was nonplussed. Then the girl said, 'You are Mr Davies?'

'How do you know my name?' asked Leo.

She held out the piece of paper with his name and address on it. Leo took it and read it. Wondering what the hell was going

160

on, he said, 'You'd better come in.'

He showed the girl into the living room and sat her down in a chair. He asked her name, and she told him.

'Where are you from? Your country?'

'Ukraine,' she replied.

'Where did you get this?' he asked her, indicating the piece of paper.

'A man – Viktor Kroitor,' she replied. The name meant nothing to Leo, but it was evident that she must in some way be connected to the creep who'd come to his house a week ago.

'Who is Viktor Kroitor?' he asked.

She swallowed hard, thinking. At length she said, 'He is man who bring me from Ukraine to here, to London. I am to be dancer here. He take my – my – my – papers – I don't know – '

'Your passport,' said Leo, beginning to get the picture.

She nodded. 'My passport.' She gulped again, fighting back tears. 'But no work. No dancer work. He keep me in hotel, and I have to – I have to – ' She floundered again, gesticulating in hopeless misery.

'He made you a prostitute,' said Leo.

'Yes – yes. I am prostitute with other girls.' She burst into tears, and Leo went to the kitchen to get her some water, hoping she wasn't going to make off with all the valuables from the living room in his absence. She seemed utterly believable, however. Was Viktor Kroitor the man who had come to threaten him? It seemed likely, if something of a coincidence.

He gave Irina the water and she drank it, and grew calmer. Leo pulled up a chair near to hers and sat down. She had begun to talk frantically in Ukrainian, and he had to stop her.

'Calm down,' he said, speaking slowly, 'I can't understand anything you say. Talk English, and tell me how you found me, how you got this piece of paper.'

'There was man at hotel. Marko. Viktor's man. He like me, he help me.'

'He got you out of the hotel?'

She nodded.

'And where is he now, this man Marko?' The last thing he wanted was yet another mad Ukrainian battering on his door tonight.

Irina shrugged and said, 'I lose him.' She sincerely hoped that Marko was enjoying a miserable time wandering the streets of London in fear of his life, but she wouldn't have said this to Leo Davies, even if she could. She dug in her bag and brought out Viktor's wallet. 'Viktor Kroitor's. I take from hotel.' She pointed to the piece of paper. 'Your name is in it. Marko say – he say Viktor come here to – to – not be nice?'

'To threaten me.' Leo nodded. So this Viktor Kroitor *was* the man who'd come here, which was why she'd found his name and address in his wallet. It made sense. Not so much of a coincidence, after all.

'So I think – you might be friend. You might help? I know nowhere else to go.' Her eyes were fastened hopefully on his face.

Leo looked inside the wallet. Who the hell carried this much cash around? Presumably only gangsters. He inspected the credit cards and put them back.

'Would you like something to eat?' he asked Irina.

She nodded hesitantly, smiling for the first time, and tears came to her eyes. 'Thank you,' she said.

Leo took her into the kitchen and made her an omelette and a cup of coffee. Gradually he learned her story – how she hadn't had enough money to carry on her studies in Odessa, how Viktor Kroitor had promised her work, and she had believed him, and what had happened to her since.

Leo made himself some coffee and watched her as she ate. So she was a part of it all. This wretched girl represented the kind of profits that Viktor Kroitor was laundering through Sir Dudley Humble's company. How many other girls had been tricked and enslaved by this man Kroitor? How much more misery did he deal in? Leo supposed that if he were a good, upstanding citizen, he would take her to the police, and let them deal with Viktor Kroitor. If they could find him.

'Do you know where the hotel is? The one where Viktor Kroitor was keeping you?' he asked Irina.

She shook her head. 'No. I don't know.'

So there was no way of leading the police straight to Kroitor. Anything could happen in the meantime. Kroitor obviously had connections and very good intelligence. If he found out Leo had taken Irina to the police, he might well carry out this threat to harm Rachel or Oliver.

Leo poured Irina another cup of coffee. On one view, she was an unfortunate young woman who ought to be taken straight to the Ukrainian Embassy and put on a plane back home. On the other hand...

Am I mad? thought Leo. Was there really anything to be gained by opening up negotiations with this criminal bastard Kroitor? He would have to think this out very carefully.

He went out to the garden, where the mid-evening September air was already chilly, and paced the lawn, keeping an occasional eye on Irina through the window, weighing up the options. It was like a legal case, he told himself, another problem with a variety of solutions. All he had to do was maximise his chances of a favourable outcome. He pondered the matter for a while, and at length decided that the answer was the usual one – to seek a settlement with the other side, if possible.

A movement caught his eye, and he glanced towards the kitchen to see Irina gesturing to him. He went inside.

'Bell,' she said, pointing to the hall in alarm. The doorbell sounded again.

Christ, thought Leo, if the situation wasn't so serious, it would be verging on the farcical. Cautiously he went to the door and looked through the spyhole. There on the doorstep stood Lola, dressed up to the nines. He opened the door.

'Leo – ' She reached up and exchanged air kisses with him. ' – I was on my way to a do in Markham Gardens, and was in danger of being uncharacteristically on time, so I thought I'd drop in and see you.' Leo opened the door wider to let her in. 'I have to tell you I'm very worried about Anthea. I don't care if you think

I'm interfering, but she's absolutely my best friend in the world, and I can't bear to see her so miserable.'

'You needn't worry about Anthea. She's upset for no reason. Her sister Lucy has been telling lies and making trouble. She admitted it to me. I've had a word with Lucy and it's going to be sorted out in the next day or two, I promise you. I texted her, saying Lucy had something to tell her. Come through and have a drink.'

'God, that kid's a monster,' said Lola, as she followed Leo into the kitchen. She began to shrug off her jacket, then paused when she saw Irina standing there. 'Oh, I'm sorry. I didn't realise you had – '

'This is Irina. I've only just made her acquaintance. Irina, this is my friend Lola.' He mixed Lola a gin-and-tonic and handed it to her. 'Sit down and hear something. You happen to have walked into one of the most grotesque situations of my life. I'd like to explain it to someone, and it might as well be you.'

And Leo, over the next ten minutes, told Lola everything that had happened to him since the day that Viktor Kroitor had come to the house. Why tell Lola? He had no idea, except that she was so extraneous to all of it, that he could think of no one better.

Irina stood listening to the incomprehensible babble of their speedy English, picking up very little of what was going on. Her feelings of loneliness and insecurity were made even more intense by being in this nice house, among these lucky people so sure of themselves and their place in the world. She had no idea what they were deciding on her behalf. Furtively she admired Lola's expensive, fashionable clothes, and beautifully manicured hands and made-up face, and each time that Lola glanced in her direction, Irina gave a nervous, tentative smile.

'My God, Leo,' said Lola, when Leo had finished. 'What a bloody awful situation. What are you going to do?' She actually thought it was pretty exciting, given how mundane life generally was.

'I was thinking about that just before you arrived. My priority is to make sure that this man Kroitor stops threatening my family. Inadvisable as it may sound, I intend to talk to him.

But in order to do that effectively, I need to have Irina tucked away safely somewhere, as a potential witness. She's my bargaining counter. I don't care about Kroitor, or what he gets up to, so long as I can make sure he stays away from me and my family. Not very public-spirited, perhaps, but there it is.'

'No, darling, I quite agree. I'm entirely on your side. But when you say 'tucked away–?'

'Viktor Kroitor must have no idea of her possible whereabouts, so she can't stay here.'

Lola gave Irina another glance. This was all so intriguing, and really rather fun. 'I suppose – ' She paused thoughtfully. 'Have you any other friends who know about this?'

'Lola, darling, I'm not asking you to have her. Don't worry.'

Lola held out her glass. 'This really is the weediest g-and-t in the world. Slosh in a little more Bombay Sapphire and I might just let her stay with me.' She caught his look of astonishment. 'Really.'

He poured her some more gin. 'Lola, I can't ask you to do that. It's bad enough for me without anyone else getting involved – '

'Oh, stop. I'd like to do something useful and interesting for a change.' She smiled at Irina. 'Do you think she's understood anything we've been talking about?'

'A bit, I suppose.' He paused. 'Lola, are you absolutely serious? Would you have her for a day or two?'

'Why not? If it'll help.'

Leo turned to Irina and spoke slowly to her. 'Listen, Irina – I want to help you to get back to the Ukraine, but first, I need to do some things. Get your passport back, for one. This lady –' He indicated Lola '– says you can stay with her for a couple of days. OK?'

Irina hesitated. She hadn't a clue what they'd been talking about earlier, except that Viktor's name had come up regularly. She didn't understand how this woman came into things, either. But she had no choice. She had to trust someone. And the woman looked nice. Probably her house was nice, too. All she really wanted was to get away from London, to get back to the Ukraine. This man Leo had said he would get her passport back. She didn't know how he was going to do that, but something in his eyes made her believe he would. She nodded at Lola and murmured, 'Thank you.'

'Are you sure?' Leo asked Lola again. 'Are you absolutely sure?'

'Absolutely. Much more fun than going to Hugo's party.' She knocked back the remains of her drink and gestured towards Irina's bag. 'Does she have any things, or is that it?'

'That's all she came with.'

'By the way,' asked Lola, as she stood up, 'how are you going to speak to this man Kroitor if you don't know where he is?'

Leo was stunned by his own lack of foresight. 'I hadn't thought of that.'

This much Irina had understood. She dived into her bag again and brought out Marko's mobile phone. She handed it to Leo. 'Is Marko's. He leave on table, and I take. Viktor's number is on it.'

Leo looked at Irina in admiration. 'Brilliant.'

'Now, Leo, darling,' said Lola, putting on her jacket, 'would you be a dear and ring for a cab?'

33

Leo spent much of the next morning weighing up the situation, going over and over the various options, uncertain what to do for the best. By lunchtime he had made up his mind. He took Marko's mobile phone from his briefcase – where it had buzzed forlornly and rather irritatingly on several occasions – and scrolled through the address book till he came to Viktor's name.

Viktor was at his Paddington flat, the one he used as a base for his London operations. He was feeling irate, to put it mildly. Last night he had lost one of his girls, along with his wallet with all his cash and credit cards, and had spent the hours since then threatening to kill that fat, useless shit Marko – who appeared to be the one responsible – in the slowest, most disgustingly excruciating way conceivable if ever he got his hands on him. So he was mildly nonplussed, when his phone rang, to see that it was apparently Marko who was calling. He stared for a moment, then answered.

'Marko! Where the – ' But the voice which interrupted him was not Marko's.

'Viktor Kroitor? I wonder if you remember me.' Viktor struggled for some seconds to tried to place the cool, familiar tones. 'You called at my house not long ago. Leo Davies.'

Davies! What the fuck was he doing with Marko's phone? He paused, collecting his thoughts as he tried to work out the implications of this bizarre development, then said, 'I remember.'

'You're no doubt a little puzzled as to why I'm calling you.'

Viktor's cooling anger was replaced by bemused suspicion. 'Tell me, Mr Davies, where did you get the phone?'

'Well, it's a long story. I don't propose to go into it right now. The reason I'm calling you, Viktor, is to arrange a meeting.

You don't mind if I call you Viktor, do you? Makes things more informal.'

Viktor laughed. This guy was mad, but he had some fucking nerve. 'Call me what you like. What do you mean – a meeting?'

'Between you and me. There are a few things we need to discuss. Irina Karpacheva, for one.'

Viktor was beginning to make some sense of this, but was struggling to work out how on earth Marko and the girl had got involved with Davies. 'What about her?'

'She's useful to you – and to me. I'd like to reach some kind of deal – what we lawyers call a settlement. I suggest some nice, neutral place – say in an hour's time? Do you know the Temple at all?'

'What's that – some kind of church?'

'No, it's an area of London, between Fleet Street and Embankment. Have you got a pen? Right – get a cab, and ask to be dropped at the bottom of Middle Temple Lane, and walk up fifty yards or so. I'll meet you. Or you could get one of your chaps to drive you – not Marko, obviously.'

Viktor, still mildly angry, had to laugh. There was a ludicrous kind of charm about this guy. 'Why should I have a meeting with you? Just say what you've got to say now. Don't waste my time.'

'I like to do things face to face. It's the best way of communicating, don't you think? Also, much as I'd love to chat, I think the battery on Marko's phone is running low. I hope you'll turn up. Given what Irina has told me, I think you should. You might even get your wallet back, in return for Irina's passport. Make sure you bring it. Oh, and before you ask, I have no intention of involving the police, or Sir Dudley, or anyone else. This is between you and me. As you said at our last meeting – strictly personal.'

Leo clicked the phone off and put it down. Would Kroitor turn up in an hour's time? As matters stood, Leo didn't see that he had a choice.

Viktor sat there, perplexed and furious. He couldn't believe it. This guy, whose family he'd threatened with harm, was coming on to him and telling him to turn up to meetings? He got up and went to the window, staring down at the street, trying to put things together. By using Marko's phone, and by saying he wanted to talk about Irina, Davies had pretty much laid it on the line. He had all he needed to go to the police. Given that Marko knew just about everything, Viktor wouldn't even have time to get to the airport before he was picked up. And that would be the end. Shit! Viktor paced the room, re-rehearsing the horrible things he would do to Marko if he ever met him again. But why would Marko do this? He stood to gain absolutely nothing by betraying Viktor. Quite the reverse. Then again, Davies had said he wasn't going to involve the police. He'd said he wanted to meet to do a deal. Did he want money, or what? These barrister people were supposed to be incorruptible and utterly honest – or so Sir Dudley said. Sir Dudley – he was the fool who'd started all this. It was his panic over that one stupid invoice which had led to Viktor visiting Davies and threatening his family. Clearly Leo Davies was not, at this moment, intimidated by those threats. Given the cards in his hand, Viktor could see why.

After a few more minutes spent musing and fuming, Viktor went to the next room and instructed one of his men to drive him to this place called the Temple.

34

A little before one, and after much cursing and arguing over the A-Z, Viktor's driver dropped Viktor off on the Embankment, at the foot of Middle Temple Lane.

'Be back here in half an hour,' said Viktor, thinking that it was time to get a new car with sat nav. He turned and began to walk up Middle Temple Lane. He was mildly impressed by, but not much interested in the stately elegance of his surroundings, being more preoccupied with what he would say and do when he met Leo Davies.

Leo, loitering by the corner of Crown Office Row, saw Viktor coming. There was no mistaking that dreadful coat. He watched as Viktor approached, waiting for the moment of recognition. There was something mundane about this encounter, here in the open, surrounded by lawyers and office workers on their lunch hour, compared to the night that Viktor had forced his way into his house. Leo sincerely hoped he could achieve enough today to make sure he never saw Viktor Kroitor in his life again.

'Let's take a walk,' said Leo.

They made an incongruous pair as they strolled along Crown Office Row – the dapper, silver-haired lawyer in his elegant pinstrip suit walking next to the big, bulky six foot four Eastern European with his hands thrust into the pockets of his leather coat. A couple of acquaintances nodded to Leo as they passed, giving his companion a curious glance. A client, they supposed.

'You said this would be neutral,' remarked Viktor. 'You seem to know a lot of people.'

'Do you feel unsafe?' asked Leo, as they approached the wrought-iron gates of Inner Temple Garden.

Viktor didn't deign to answer this. He walked with Leo through the gates and into the ornate, spacious gardens. They found a bench and sat down.

Viktor lit a cigarette, and blew a casual plume of smoke into the bright September air. 'How is Sir Dudley's case going?' he asked.

Surprised by the insouciance of this enquiry, Leo replied, 'It's proceeding. I imagine we'll win. I wouldn't have thought you'd be interested in that aspect of Sir Dudley's business.'

Viktor narrowed his eyes and smiled. 'You think you know everything that's going on, don't you?'

'Hardly. But I know enough.'

Viktor smoked for a few seconds. 'So, this deal you wanted to talk about – ' He paused, giving Leo an appraising glance. 'You don't look like a man who cuts deals, I have to tell you.'

'I do it every day for a living,' replied Leo. 'It's all a question of negotiating the obstacles, finding a way to the result you want. I imagine you know all about that, in your line of work, though you probably use a little less finesse than I do.'

'Finesse? What is that? Tell me – I like to know new words.'

'Subtlety. Sophistication.'

Viktor laughed and nodded. 'OK.' He took a final drag of his cigarette and ground it beneath his shoe. 'Now, tell me your deal.'

'I've brought you here to extract from you a promise – a promise that you will stay away from my son and his mother, never to threaten them, or me, in your life again. Forget they exist.'

'And if I promise to do this – you give me the girl Irina and that son-of-a-bitch Marko? Is this your deal?'

'The deal is that if you *don't* agree, then I solemnly promise you I will bust Sir Dudley wide open – and if I do that, you and your operation are unlikely to survive very long, knowing Sir Dudley.'

Leo had no idea how Viktor was going to respond to this. He seemed neither angry nor surprised. He just sat there in silence for a few moments. Then he nodded and said, 'Sir Dudley gives me a lot of problems. He gives me grief – is that what you say?'

'That's what we say.'

Viktor met Leo's disconcertingly clear gaze. Despite his undemonstrative manner and conservative appearance, there was a ruthless and uncompromising quality about Leo which intrigued Viktor. It commanded his respect. 'I don't get this. I don't get this at all. If you are so sure, if you know so much, why don't you just go to the police?'

'Because to be honest, Viktor, you frighten me. I don't for one minute believe that if I were to go to the police, and they were to pick you up, that it would end there. You'd find a way to carry out your threats, or get someone to carry out your threats for you. I would have an enemy for life, and I can do without that. Frankly, I don't care about your sordid operations, or your criminal activities. I just want to be kept out of them, and to keep my family out of them. Not the attitude of a responsible citizen, perhaps, but I care more about their safety than what you do for a living. I don't like you, but I'd rather stay on your side. Do you follow me?'

'I follow.' Viktor chuckled. 'You are an interesting man. But you know what? If you were ever to carry out your threat to bust Sir Dudley, and the police found their way to me – ' Viktor shrugged.

'You've arrived very neatly at the point. Our interests are perfectly balanced. As is the way with all good settlements, it depends upon both parties respecting their sides of the bargain. You stay away from my family, and I do nothing about Sir Dudley.'

'But for this deal to work, I need to know where Irina and Marko are. I want them.'

'I don't know anything about Marko, except that he's clearly none too bright. He helped Irina to get out of the hotel, and then she dumped him. The reason she found her way to me is because my name and address were in your wallet, which she took, along with Marko's phone. As for Irina herself her – well, she's another of my bargaining tools, but not in the way you seem to think. She's somewhere you can't find her for the moment, but once I have your word and her passport, she'll be straight on a plane back to the Ukraine.' Viktor made an angry sound of impatience, and Leo dipped his hand into his pocket. 'Come on, what's one prostitute more or less to you, Viktor? I'd have thought your wallet and credit cards were worth more.' He took out Viktor's wallet and held it up.

Viktor hesitated, then put out his hand.

'Her passport,' Leo reminded him.

Viktor sighed grimly. 'OK – let the girl go.' He reached into his inside pocket and pulled out Irina's passport. He handed it to Leo, who gave him his wallet in return. 'You're right, Marko was always a dumb prick,' said Viktor, frowning thoughtfully at the wallet. Then he turned to Leo and said, 'You know what I think? I came here thinking you were the problem. Now I think the problem – the real problem – is Sir Dudley.' He shook his head. 'He's not a reliable trading partner. He started this, with his stupid invoice. Then he tried to tell me it was my fault, but it was his people. I know that. You – ' he jabbed a finger at Leo ' – you never wanted to get mixed up in this. I understand that.' Viktor put the wallet away, pulled out another cigarette and lit it. 'Anyway,' he went on conversationally, 'I've been thinking. There are better ways of moving money than using Sir Dudley. Ways that are less clumsy. Internet gambling – it's legal in Britain now. That's a way.'

'How would that work?' asked Leo. He was fascinated by the complexities of Viktor's character – evidently regarding himself as something of a sophisticate, a man of the world, yet at the same time exhibiting an almost puerile candour in relation to his criminal dealings.

'OK,' explained Viktor, with some modest pride in his scheme, 'you open a gambling account, put money in under a false name, then you make a few small bets. After a while you withdraw the money.' He shrugged. 'Or maybe you just open an account and store funds for a few months, then transfer the money to a clean account, pretend it's winnings.'

Leo reflected that it was going to turn out to be something of an embarrassment for the government to find that its gambling reforms were facilitating criminal activity and money laundering. Still, the best laid schemes would always provide opportunities to enterprising individuals, and without doubt Viktor Kroitor was one of those.

'I don't know why I tell you this,' remarked Viktor as an afterthought.

Leo didn't either, but he replied, 'Because we have an understanding. And perhaps because, fundamentally, our professional ethics aren't so very disparate.'

'Disparate – what is that?'

'It means different, far apart. Take prostitution, for instance – that's one of your rackets. The work I do as a barrister isn't so far removed from prostitution.'

Viktor frowned. 'How is that?'

'Oh – ' Leo gave a sigh, glancing around at the lawyers strolling through the gardens ' – the degradation of applying one's intellect to say what one doesn't necessarily believe, much of the time. Doing for money the most unacceptable things for the most unacceptable people.'

Viktor smiled and shook his head. 'You're a funny guy.' He stood up, dusting cigarette ash carefully from his leather coat.

'So,' said Leo, 'have we a deal? Do you give me your promise?'

Viktor shrugged. 'OK, you have your deal. Like I said – Sir Dudley is my problem, not yours.'

They walked back in silence to the gates of the garden, and Viktor, glancing round, observed, 'You work in a nice place. A beautiful place.'

'Yes,' agreed Leo. 'It is.'

Without another word Viktor walked back down Middle Temple Lane towards the Embankment, and the last Leo saw of him he was standing by the busy roadside, cigarette in hand, scanning the road for his driver and his car.

35

Leo went back into the gardens, past the neatly clipped lawns and well-tended beds of glorious late summer flowers. He sat down again on a bench, letting the warmth of the September sun creep into his skin and bones, drinking in the elusive fragrance of the roses. As he looked round the gardens, he wondered idly what kind of day it had been six centuries ago, when Richard Plantagenet and the Earls of Suffolk and Warwick, having become embroiled in argument in Inner Temple Hall, had come out to these same gardens and plucked the red and white roses which had become symbols of their factions before the commencement of the Wars of the Roses. Had it been a mellow day such as this one, or in the bright heat of early summer? His knowledge of history was insufficiently particular. He wondered, too, if the gardens had looked so very different then. Somewhat, he supposed – much larger, with the Thames waters lapping at their lower reaches in the days before a river wall was built, or the Embankment conceived of, but still a calm, fragrant retreat from the noisome hubbub of the busy streets.

Leo closed his eyes and let his thoughts wander over the events which had troubled 5 Caper Court over the last few days. It was a burdensome business, being head of chambers, but he wasn't sure he was quite ready to relinquish it yet. The sounds of the city, like those of a constant tide, rose around him. He opened his eyes and looked around. The greatest and deepest of London's many qualities, he had long since decided, was the sense of rolling history with which it was imbued. Buildings rose and crumbled, people lived and died, institutions grew and dwindled, yet the city carried on relentlessly, the changes and erosions of the passing ages only serving to mark more deeply the pattern of its story. It made sense that Pudding Lane, that tiny vennel of history, was no more now than a lifeless alley flanked by the vast concrete walls of office buildings. Its meagre length, the repository of great events, had endured, but the city made no concessions; its was too busy with its own teeming, ever-shifting progress. This place where he now sat, the buildings round him, were part of that history, and he was as well, in his insignificant way. At any rate, he was as long as he lived and worked here, as long as his name was still listed among those of the other tenants on the hand-painted board outside 5 Caper Court.

He rose and strolled to the foot of the gardens and along the broad gravel walk – so old it had even been mentioned by Shakespeare – then across the grass towards the pond and the statue of the little boy which stood as a memorial to Charles Lamb. The pond had been rebuilt in the millennium year, and a fountain added, and Leo reflected that its bright waters might still be splashing in the bright air two hundred years hence, and seem as much a part of the Inn's history as the rest of it. The little boy in the statue was holding an open book – although he had passed it many times, Leo had never looked to see what might be written on its pages. He did so now, and saw Thackeray's words engraved there: '*Lawyers I suppose were children once.*'

He walked back round the gardens, and by the time he had reached the gates once more, he had decided that he had no real wish to join Roger in his virtual chambers, with its efficient working practices, its members toiling away in the seclusion of their own ambitions for greater profits, their working days shorn of the pleasures of a place such as this. What would his working life be, after all, without the stimulus of the Temple and its inhabitants, and the beauty of its buildings, courts and gardens? It would be work and no more, and solitary work at that. No, thought Leo, Oliver would have to forego the pleasure of being picked up by his father each day from school. He wasn't ready to jack this all in just yet.

He glanced at his watch, saw it was ten to two, and went back to chambers. Anthony was returning to his room with a cup of coffee as Leo came upstairs, looking subdued.

'You OK?' Anthony asked him.

'Sort of. Remember that Ukrainian I told you about – the one who came to the house? I've just been taking a stroll round Inner Temple Gardens with him.'

'Good God,' said Anthony, opening his door. 'Come in and tell me about it.'

Leo sat down in a chair opposite Anthony's desk and told him about Irina's arrival at his house, and his meeting with Viktor Kroitor.

'I don't understand,' said Anthony. 'Why didn't you just call the police?'

'I had no idea of his whereabouts. The girl Irina was pretty much disoriented – she had no idea where she'd been kept. All I had was this mobile phone which the girl gave me. At least it was a way of getting hold of him.'

'But the police might have been able to trace him through the phone. I don't know. Or maybe if you'd let them speak to the girl – '

'Oh, for Christ's sake, Anthony! Don't you understand? I don't care about Viktor Kroitor! I don't care whether he's selling girls, drugs or AK42 rifles! I only care about my son, and putting a stop to the threats to his safety. Christ, ever since that conference on Monday with Sir Dudley, when I indicated that I knew what he was up to – '

'I told you – you did the right thing.'

Leo gave an irritable sigh. 'So you've already said. But it was only later that I realised that I'd put the wind up Sir Dudley, and that I might just have achieved the opposite of what I'd intended. What if he told Viktor Kroitor to do as he'd threatened? I had to talk to Kroitor, to convince him he had everything to lose.'

'And did you?'

'Yes – I think so. Kroitor doesn't work for Sir Dudley. As I had suspected, it's rather the other way round, though they have shared interests. He uses Sir Dudley's company – or companies – to launder his criminal profits. He's by no means a stupid man.

I've pretty much made him see that I'm irrelevant. In fact, I get the impression that it's Sir Dudley he blames for jeopardising affairs.'

'Oh dear.'

Leo shrugged. 'I don't care. Just as I don't care about Kroitor.' His eyes met Anthony's. 'You think that's immoral, don't you? You think I've shirked my duty to help put a stop to organised crime by putting my interests first.' He rose from his chair with a sigh. 'I don't know what's bloody well right or wrong these days. I just know I want to get on with my life in peace.' He paced the room for a moment, detesting the silence, and the sense that Anthony was judging him. At last he said, 'Oh for God's sake – say what you think.'

Mildly surprised, Anthony replied, 'I'm sorry, I was thinking about something else entirely. I was thinking about Roger's proposal, and wondering if you'd come to a decision yet. But you probably haven't had time to think about it, with all that's been going on – '

'No, no,' sighed Leo, 'I've been thinking about it in the last half hour, as it happens.'

'And?'

'I don't think I'm going to buy into it, after all. They all see it as an escape, a way of avoiding all the unsatisfactory aspects of chambers life. But that means leaving behind all the good things – things which don't necessarily manifest themselves in terms of money or efficiency. This place, for instance. This world. I like it too much. I like talking to people, and seeing them every day. I like seeing you.' He glanced at Anthony's face, unable to decipher his expression. 'What? Are you disappointed?'

'In a way.' Anthony hesitated. 'I had this idea, you see – OK, probably utterly ridiculous – ' He stopped again, evidently mildly embarrassed.

'Go on. Tell me.'

'Well, I had this idea that if we left Caper Court and joined Roger's virtual chambers, that we might work together. Be together. You and I.' His eyes met Leo's.

'It would be nice,' said Leo. How inadequate the words were. How ridiculously paltry as a means of expressing how much he would have liked to share his entire world with Anthony. But such a step, such an enormous emotional and physical step, would destroy the fragile compromise with Rachel, who had the power to remove Oliver from his life for good, if she chose to. It wasn't a risk he could ever afford to take, no matter how much he might have wanted to. 'It would have been nice, I mean. But as things are – ' Leo moved away from the window, aware that he mustn't, above all, let this become a moment of weakness. ' – the status quo must prevail, I'm afraid.'

Anthony nodded. He had just about laid his heart on the line. Leo's pragmatic response had left him numb. 'Of course.'

'Anyway, I have to get on. See you about.'

Leo left the room. He stood on the landing for some moments, listening to the various sounds of chambers – a door closing somewhere, Peter whistling as he went downstairs with a stack of briefs, the faint sound of two of the girls talking as they made coffee in the kitchen – and fought the urge to go back into Anthony's room and say, yes. Yes, come and be with me, work with me, exist with me. Love me. No good, he thought at last. No good. Where Anthony was concerned, it was all too little or not enough.

After a few moments he turned and went upstairs to his room. Too much of the day had been spent on other business. He had to get some work done before the chambers' meeting at half five.

36

The chambers' meeting was to be held in one of the conference rooms, and barristers began to drift in shortly before five, chatting and finding seats. Leo was just about to leave his room to go and chair the meeting, when Henry knocked. He handed Leo an envelope. 'Mr Faber asked me to give you this, sir.'

'Thank you, Henry.'

When Henry had left, Leo opened the envelope and read its contents. Then he folded it up, slipped it into his jacket pocket, and went to the conference room.

'Are we all here?' asked Leo, taking his seat and slipping on his spectacles as he glanced round the long, oval table.

'All except Maurice,' said Simon.

'Maurice won't be joining us,' said Leo. He took the letter from his pocket. 'I received his letter of resignation just a moment ago.' A murmur of consternation rippled round the room. 'I shall read it to you.'

Leo read out the letter; its contents were perfunctory, and its tone amiable and unapologetic. Maurice said that in the light of recent events he had decided that it would be in the best interests of chambers if he were to resign, that he had much enjoyed his time at 5 Caper Court, and that he wished everyone well for the future.

Leo folded the letter up. 'In the light of this I don't see any point in dwelling on the events of the past few days. Suffice to say that the relevant committees will meet to deal with outstanding issues relating to Maurice's finances. In the meantime, there is the matter of the unauthorised access by one member of chambers of another member's computer. 'Leo cast a glance in Roger's direction. 'Roger, I think you have something to say to us?'

Henry and Felicity glanced up expectantly as Leo came into the clerks' room half an hour later. He came over to where they were working and sat on the edge of Felicity's desk.

'Well, that's that,' he told them. 'Maurice has resigned.'

'What? At the meeting?'

'He didn't attend. He gave Henry a letter.'

'I had a hunch about that letter,' observed Henry. 'He gave it me as he was going out at lunchtime. I said, 'By the way, sir, are there any other matters we should know about?' He knew I was talking about those fee notes. He gave me such a look.'

'Cheeky sod,' said Felicity. 'I'm surprised he's resigned, though. I thought he had all kinds of excuses?'

'All kinds, and all somewhat bogus,' said Leo. 'I think he knew his position was untenable.'

Felicity leaned her chin on her hand. 'He'd got a nerve, billing direct like that. Then again, I'm sometimes amazed you lot don't do more of it. I mean, if Mr Fry hadn't done what he did, no one would have known. How much did it all add up to? Half a million nearly, wasn't it?'

'If we all just looked out for our own self-interest, the whole point of chambers would collapse. It's a team game. Maurice forgot that.'

'He's a stirrer, anyway. He's made more trouble round here than you know about, Mr Davies,' said Felicity darkly.

'Well, he won't any more. By the way, what happened to that application notice I gave you earlier? It needs to be served by Monday.'

'Right on top of it, Mr D,' said Felicity briskly.

A few moments later Leo was checking the contents of his pigeon hole when Anthony came into the clerks' room.

'That was an interesting little meeting, wasn't it?'

'Something of a surprise, Maurice resigning so quickly,' said Leo.

'Someone said there have been rumours that he's been in talks with Matrix Chambers for a while now.'

'Double hearsay, Anthony – you know how unreliable that is.'

'I'll bet it's true, though. He hasn't been happy since he lost the vote on becoming head of chambers last year.'

'He's been a difficult man to live with, certainly. But I'll miss his expertise on the marketing side of things. We'll need to find someone else to take that on.' Leo reflected for a moment. 'Do you suppose Roger and the others would have become so restless if it hadn't been for Maurice?'

'I don't think it would have made any difference. They're pretty much set on this virtual chambers project. I hadn't expected Roger to lay his cards on the table at today's meeting, though.'

'I think he felt it was timely,' said Leo. 'More than a few members of chambers thought that going into Maurice's computer was pretty reprehensible. Personally, I thought it was merely daft.' He glanced at Anthony. 'Still no second thoughts about joining them?'

Anthony met his gaze. 'You know I haven't. I'm happy here.'

'Good,' nodded Leo. 'Good.' There was a pause. 'Free for a drink?'

'Absolutely.'

37

That evening Anthea went to see Lola. She hadn't heard from Leo since Wednesday evening, when she'd hung up on him, and although she'd told him that she never wanted to see him in her life again, she had expected him to make a bit more effort. But there had simply been silence. She'd had thoughts of going round and gouging Lucy's evil eyes out with one of her school pencils but, cathartic and pleasurable as such an act might be, it would also constitute an acknowledgement that her own younger sister had managed to rob, crush, humiliate and hurt her, and she was not prepared openly to concede this, certainly not in front of their mother.

So she repaired to Lola's in search of the customary comforts, and took as a present for her friend a nifty Marc Jacobs dress which she'd been given as a freebie at a fashion shoot that day. Possibly a little on the small side, but Lolly might as well try it on.

She arrived at Lola's penthouse to find Lola and a very pretty dark-haired girl watching a re-run of *Catwalk* on Sky.

Lola kissed her friend, then made introductions. 'Ant, darling, this is Irina. I met her at Leo's house. She's staying with me for a couple of days. Irina, this is Anthea – she's Leo's girlfriend.'

Irina shook Anthea's slim, cool hand. 'You are lucky,' she said tentatively. 'He is lovely man.'

'Not the word I would use,' said Anthea, still busy unravelling Lola's introduction. 'And I'm not his girlfriend – not any more.' She turned to Lola. 'What d'you mean, you met her at Leo's house? Is this another one he hasn't told me about?' Anthea gave a little sigh of confusion and despair and handed Lola the Marc

Jacob's bag. 'Here, this is for you. Have you got any wine open? I need a drink.' She sank down on a sofa, kicking off her shoes and stretching out her legs.

'Darling, thank you – I'll open it in a moment. I thought you'd have spoken to Leo by now. He said it was all sorted out.' Lola disappeared in the direction of the kitchen, calling out, 'Shall we have some shampers? It is Friday, after all.' She reappeared a moment later with a chilled bottle of Tattinger, one of a stack she kept in the fridge. Irina stared in astonishment. How rich this girl was! She'd already had a tour of Lola's enormous walk-in closet and marvelled at the racks of expensive clothes and shoes.

'What do you mean – all sorted out?' said Anthea. 'I haven't spoken to him since I saw you. When did you see him?' Her eyes strayed in the direction of the television. 'D'you think Liz Hurley's had a boob job?'

'No – not perky enough. Last night. Hold on – I'll get some glasses. You pop the cork.'

Irina watched as Anthea wedged the bottle between her slim thighs and prised the cork out with practised ease. Lola came back with glasses and set them out on the coffee table, grinning at Irina. 'Isn't this fun? Anthea and I find any old excuse for shampers.' She poured the champagne, continuing to Anthea, 'Leo told me Lucy had admitted to him she'd been lying her head off – like *that*'s unusual – and that he'd sent you a text. Haven't you spoken to her?'

'I haven't spoken to anyone. I've been too miserable. My God, I was a wreck today – the make-up artist had to use about a gallon of Touche Éclat. Anyway, I deleted his text without reading it. I knew it was just him trying to get off the hook.'

'Well, give the man a chance! He said you should talk to Lucy.'

'Talk to that little bitch? As if.'

Irina had been sitting mystified, unable to follow the speed of their chatter. Anthea caught her dazed expression and lifted her glass in Irina's direction. 'Cheers, sweetie. Don't look so

184

stunned. What's her name again? Irina. OK, here's to you, Irina.' Then Anthea turned to Lola. 'You still haven't told me how you came to meet her at Leo's.'

Lola swallowed a hasty mouthful of champagne. 'You are *not* going to believe this story!' And she recounted everything which Leo had told her, with a few embellishments, with Irina nodding away in confirmation of such parts as she could understand.

When Lola had finished, Anthea gazed at Irina in shock and pity. 'Oh, you poor girl! That is so horrible! What did Leo say he was going to do?'

Irina shrugged. 'He say he get my passport.'

'I can't imagine how he thinks he's going to do that,' murmured Anthea.

They discussed the matter for some time, pouring out glasses of champagne, asking Irina questions about her home, and her life before London. 'Darling,' said Anthea, 'you truly don't want to work as a cabaret dancer. I mean, truly, *truly*.'

'Is lot of money,' said Irina. 'I need money to study.'

'What were you studying – before you came here?'

'Medicine. Is very expensive. I cannot buy books.'

Lola and Anthea exchanged glances. 'Well,' said Lola, 'books can't cost much more than champagne. I think you should go back and try to finish your studies.' She picked up the empty bottle and shook it, then noticed the Marc Jacobs bag. 'Oh, let's see what you brought me!' She took out the dress and held it up. 'Ant, it's divine! What size is it? Oh God! I can't get into a ten, you know I can't.' She glanced at Irina. 'I'll bet you're a ten, Irina. Would you like to try it on?'

Irina smiled and nodded. 'Go on, then – hop off to the bedroom and slip it on.'

A few minutes later Irina came back in the dress, which fitted beautifully.

'Baby, it's yours,' said Lola. 'In fact – ' She got up. 'Come on – I'm going to raid my wardrobe and give you every size ten I've got. Time I gave up pretending I'm going to diet and get into them one day.'

They went through to Lola's closet and spent some time culling Lola's vast wardrobe of items bought in her many optimistic moments. 'There you are,' said Lola to Irina, who stood with heaps of garments over either arm. 'The triumph of hope over experience, that lot.'

'For me?' asked Irina.

'Most definitely. I'll find you a suitcase to take them all back home in.'

She glanced at the rails of her closet. 'All I have to do now is go shopping and fill the gaps.'

'What are you going to do about Leo?' asked Lola, when they were back on the sofa once more.

'I don't know,' said Anthea. 'Do you really think it's possible Lucy was making it all up?

'Darling, she's admitted it!'

'Not to me.'

'Well, that's why you should talk to her. I'm surprised you ever believed a word she said. Certainly Leo seemed pretty calm about it all. Go and see her.'

'Yes?'

'Yes.'

'Right, I will.' She picked up her bag and her jacket. 'What are you two going to do?'

'Have supper, Ukrainian style. Irina is going to make nylysnyky – that's crepes. Possibly accompanied by some chilled horilka.'

'Horilka?'

'Vodka – what else?'

'Crepes and vodka. Yuck.' She turned and smiled at Irina. 'Well, look, if I don't see you again – best of luck.' She leaned down and gave Irina two light, fragrant kisses, then went home to try to comb out the tangles of her love life.

38

Anthea went round to South Kensington and found Lucy at home alone, as usual, dressed in an old pair of combats, a baggy sweatshirt, and slipper socks.

'Where's mother?' asked Anthea.

'She's out with her new man.' Lucy regarded Anthea with sullen apprehension. She'd been meaning to talk to her, after the things Leo had said, but she hadn't had the guts. It looked as though there was no avoiding it now.

Anthea folded her arms and gazed at Lucy. 'I understand you have something to tell me.'

Lucy said nothing, but turned and padded through to the kitchen. Anthea followed her. Lucy perched on a stool at the breakfast bar and began to pick at a bowl of nuts.

'Well?' asked Anthea.

Lucy glanced at her sister, wishing she didn't have to stand there looking so bloody immaculate, all tall and sleek and lovely, giving her dagger looks, waiting. She toyed briefly with the idea of sticking to her original lie, but the idea faded as quickly as it had come. She shoved a hazelnut in her mouth and said, 'That stuff I told you about me and Leo, it wasn't true.'

'I can't hear you, mumbling with your mouth full of nuts.'

Lucy swallowed. 'I didn't sleep with Leo.'

Anthea took a deep breath and sat down on a stool at the breakfast bar next to Lucy. 'I see. Well, that's a start. But something happened. I want to know what, exactly.'

Lucy slumped forward, elbows on the breakfast bar, and gave a groaning sigh. After a moment she said, 'I got pissed at a club. Mum was away, and so were you. Georgia found Leo's number on my mobile and rang him, asked him to come and get me.'

'How did you happen to have his number?'

'I don't know. I just did.' Lucy paused. 'Actually,' she admitted, 'I got it off your phone.'

'Why?'

Lucy shrugged. 'I dunno.'

There was a long silence, at the end of which Anthea said, 'Did you set it up? Did you deliberately get Leo to take you back to his house?'

Lucy leaned her chin on her forearms. This was so humiliating. She frowned at the bowl of nuts, unable to look at Anthea. 'No. Sort of.'

'I think I'm beginning to understand.' There was another long silence, during which Anthea tapped her long nails on the breakfast counter.

Suddenly Lucy said, in a low, sulky voice, 'And I only knew what his sheets and stuff were like because I went and had a look. OK?'

Appalled though Anthea was at the thought that Lucy had deliberately set out to seduce Leo, she also felt a little sorry for the kid, being so infatuated and going to such lengths. And all for nothing. She felt dreadful that she hadn't believed Leo, but immensely relieved that Lucy had made it all up. There was definitely something about Leo which had made it all horribly believable.

'Lucy, you've made so much trouble – do you know that?' Anthea sounded sad and exasperated, rather than angry.

Tears welled up in Lucy's eyes, and she wiped them on her sweatshirt sleeve. 'Soz,' she mumbled. 'Sorry. Whatever.'

Anthea got up and went to make coffee for them both. She came back to the breakfast bar and set a cup down in front of Lucy, who was still sitting in her attitude of utter abjection. 'Look,' said Anthea, 'the best thing is if we both forget all about it. It was a stupid thing to do, and a stupid lie to tell, but I don't think you'll ever do anything like it again. Will you?'

Lucy shook her head.

They sipped their coffee in silence for a few moments, then Anthea said, 'So, do you want to tell me how everything's going at school?'

For half an hour Lucy let Anthea play the role of concerned, caring older sister, until a kindly balance had been restored – one in which Anthea felt pretty much back in control, and Lucy's sense of humiliation had receded.

'I have to go,' said Anthea, when she had finished her coffee.

She was going to see Leo, Lucy knew, and they were going to talk about her and the lies she'd told. Her sense of mortification returned. 'Listen,' she said, following Anthea to the front door, 'don't talk about me to Leo – OK? I can't bear the idea. I mean, I'm really sorry and everything. Please don't.'

'Oh, heavens,' said Anthea, running her fingers lightly through Lucy's messy hair as she gazed at her. 'Look at you. Your hair's a mess, your clothes look awful. How would you like to come up to town with me next week, and have a makeover? Oh, and I can blag some tickets for London Fashion Week, if you and Georgia want to come. Would you like that?'

Lucy smiled and nodded. 'And Ant?' she said, as Anthea opened the door.

'What?'

'Can I still come round to your after school sometimes?'

'Sometimes. But only if you leave my vodka alone. Promise?'

'Promise.'

Anthea dug in her bag. 'Here's your key back. And be good from now on.'

Lucy nodded. She watched Anthea go, then closed the door and went to ring Georgia and tell her the good news about the tickets for London Fashion Week.

39

During the time that Anthea was at Lola's and then with Lucy, Leo and Anthony had gone for a drink, and on to dinner. Leo was in a strange mood. Relief from anxiety had produced a sense of recklessness, but at the same time Maurice's resignation and the defection of Roger and others had left him feeling disturbed and uneasy. He needed a means of escape from himself and his preoccupations. He downed a large Scotch, and he and Anthony shared a couple of bottles of Gevrey-Chambertin Premier Cru over dinner, and had a long, intense conversation on a rambling range of topics, from Welsh rugby to the comparative merits of Eric Clapton and Carlos Santana. By half nine Leo was feeling utterly relaxed, a little drunk and powerfully aware of a restored sense of intimacy between himself and Anthony.

'We haven't done this in a long time,' said Leo. 'I can't remember the last occasion we had dinner together.'

'Neither can I. But I can tell you something else we haven't done for a while – and that's have a game of squash. I'm seriously out of condition.'

'Let's book one for next week. Stephen and I played a couple of games the week before last,' said Leo, 'but I simply haven't had the time since then. A number of pressing preoccupations.'

'How are things with Rachel?'

'As regards Oliver, you mean?' Leo signalled to the waiter for the bill. 'Fine. We had lunch, sorted a few things out. I'm supposed to have him this weekend, but she's taking him to some friends in Hampshire tomorrow. I'll have him on Sunday.' He thought about that afternoon that Viktor Kroitor had turned up at Oliver's school, and reflected that things might have been very different if she'd found out about that. He had to trust that

Viktor Kroitor would stick to their deal. 'The one thing which could have swung me towards joining Roger and the others was the idea that I might have more time to spend with Oliver. But I'm going to make a greater effort to do more work away from chambers in future.'

The bill arrived, and Leo picked it up.

'Please,' said Anthony, 'can we split it?'

'No, I'll get this. I'd like to. Reminds me of the days when you were a penniless pupil, and it was my great delight to take you out and buy you decent dinners and the odd glass of wine.'

'I was easily impressed.'

'I should hope you still are.'

Leo paid the bill and they left the restaurant. As they walked to the street corner on the lookout for taxis, Leo was suddenly conscious that he didn't want Anthony to go just yet. 'It's early,' he said. 'Come back for coffee. You still haven't seen the new place. Not so new any more.'

Anthony hesitated for a fraction of a second, then nodded. 'OK.'

At the house Leo made coffee, and poured brandies for both of them. Anthony was studying one of the pieces of art on the wall when Leo handed him his glass.

'Thanks.' Anthony took a sip of brandy and pointed at the painting. 'That reminds me of one you used to have in the house in Oxford. I remember being very struck by it the night I stayed there.'

'It's still there. This is a sister piece. How discerning of you to connect them, after all this time.'

'I remember everything about that visit. Things of that kind make a very deep impression, when one's young.'

'One doesn't have to be young.' Standing this close to Anthony, Leo was suddenly aware of profound and overwhelming desire. The familiar lines of the young man's body and face as he gazed at the painting made Leo want to reach out and touch him. Just half an hour ago in the restaurant he'd been reflecting on the necessity of maintaining a tidy private life for the satisfaction of Rachel, and ensuring the continuity of his contact with Oliver. Now such considerations vanished utterly. He lifted his hand and his fingers grazed Anthony's neck. Anthony turned and met his gaze.

'It never stops,' said Leo quietly.

'I know.' Anthony dipped his head slightly to let Leo's hand touch his face, keeping his eyes fixed on Leo's.

The sense of physicality between them was intense. 'This is something else we haven't done in a long time,' said Leo.

Anthony put up his hand to grasp Leo's. 'I'll never forget what you said after last time. Never. You said – your very words were, 'It's only sex.' That was all it was for you. But it has to be about more than that, Leo.'

'It's always been about more, where you're concerned. I was just too afraid to admit it.'

After she left Lucy, Anthea rang Leo's mobile a couple of times, but got no reply. She thought of leaving a message, but in the circumstances it was hard to know what to say. She took a taxi home, ran a bath, lit some candles, and lay soaking and exfoliating, and fantasising about seeing Leo later. She'd get him on his mobile eventually, and then he'd come round, and they would have the most wonderful sex – making-up sex was always the best – and everything would be perfect again. She could pick up where she'd left off in the tricky process of making herself and Leo an item of greater permanence.

When the fantasies and the hot water had dried up, Anthea got out, towelled herself down, stroked on some very subtle Jo Malone body lotion, and put on a simple silk caftan, which clung to her slender body in all the right places when she moved, and would be deliciously easy for Leo to take off. Glancing at the bedside clock, she saw it was a little after half ten. She went to her bag, fished out her phone, and tried Leo's mobile number again.

Leo's mobile phone was in his briefcase on the other side of the room. He could hear its insistent tone from where he stood, next to Anthony.

'Hadn't you better answer it?' asked Anthony, relinquishing Leo's hand. 'It might be important.'

Leo crossed the room and took out the phone. He saw Anthea's name on the screen, and for a moment was tempted not to answer it. But he knew she'd only ring till she got him. Better now than later.

'Anthea?'

'Hi.' Her voice sounded apprehensive. 'How are you?'

'I'm fine.'

'You sound a bit edgy.'

'Just a little tired. It's been a difficult week.'

'Darling, I'm sorry. I know that's partly been my fault. I spoke to Lucy tonight. I know what happened, and I'm so, so sorry. She's a little witch. I should never have believed her.'

'That's all right. It doesn't matter.'

'No, but I said all those dreadful things. Can you forgive me?'

'I suppose you thought you had good reason. Of course I forgive you. I'm sorry, too – the whole mess was partly my fault.'

'No, it wasn't. I blame Lucy entirely – though not for having a crush on you. That's utterly understandable. But now that it's all sorted out, I wondered – ' He could hear her smiling on the other end of the phone, her voice teasing and seductive. ' – I wondered if you'd like to come round, and we can make up properly. In bed.'

Leo glanced across the room at Anthony. 'The thing is, Anthea, I'm really exhausted. We've had some problems in chambers, a few late meetings, that kind of thing – '

'So that's why I couldn't get hold of you. In which case, you definitely need me to soothe it all away. You must be dying to see me – I know I'm absolutely aching for you.' And she went on to describe exactly how she felt, what she was wearing, what she wanted to do – till in the end Leo had to stop her.

'Seriously, I'd love to. But I think the best thing I can do is get a good night's sleep.'

'Oh.' She sounded a little piqued. 'Oh well, if that's what you think. Still – ' Her voice softened. ' – if you change your mind, I'm here all night.'

'OK. Look, I'll call you soon.' He paused. 'Night.'

Leo switched his phone off. He didn't want any more calls. Anthony was watching him from the other side of the room.

'Your girlfriend?'

'Yes.'

Anthony crossed the room, and Leo took his face between his hands and kissed him for a long, long moment.

Anthea chucked the phone on to the bed with a little sigh of disappointment. Leo really had sounded tired – a bit out of it, in fact. Probably just as well he wasn't coming over. It might all have been a bit of an anti-climax. Better to wait till he'd recharged his batteries. She flopped on to the bed, propped herself up on some pillows, and clicked on the TV with the remote. She was pretty tired herself. She lay idly watching Jonathan Ross, reflecting on the brief conversation with Leo. She shouldn't have sounded so keen. She was breaking all the rules she'd set for herself a few weeks ago. More of the hard-to-get-stuff, that was what was needed. The trouble was, it was difficult to play by those rules when you were in love.

40

'What now?' asked Leo.

'What now?' Anthony drained his coffee cup and reached for his tie. 'I think we both know the answer to that.' His tone was pragmatic, but not unkind. 'We carry on as we always have done. I don't think there's any need to make more of it than that, do you?'

Leo leaned against the kitchen worktop in his dressing-gown, studying Anthony's face. He could detect nothing in Anthony's manner of the insecurity and neediness which he had exhibited last time they had been together as lovers. 'I'm not sure about that any more,' he replied.

'Well, I am. Everything we already have is enough. We see one another just about every day. I can talk to you whenever I want. If we try to turn this into some grand passion, I know where it'll end. I've seen what happens with your relationships, and what you do to people, whether you mean to or not. I don't intend to let it happen with you and me. Anyway, weren't you the one who said he never intended to get emotionally entangled with anyone ever again?'

There was a silence, then Leo said, 'I'd give up a good deal for you, you know.'

'Well, don't. That would be fatal. Having one person in your life is never enough for you, Leo. I don't ever want to be in a position where I feel possessive, or jealous.'

'You want your freedom.'

Anthony picked up his jacket and slipped it on, hesitating before he spoke. 'Yes. Yes, if you like – that's what I want.'

Leo walked with Anthony to the front door. He smiled sadly. 'You've grown up a lot.'

'I had to.'

'I had the idea we could have spent the day together, maybe – '

'No, that's not a good idea. Anyway, I have a few things to do. I'm sure you do, too. I'll see you on Monday.'

Leo, as he shaved and showered later, reflected on the things he needed to do that day. Book a flight for Irina, give her her passport, take her to the airport, and impress upon her that if she wanted to do anything about Viktor Kroitor, she should do it in the Ukraine. He would have to thank Lola, too. And he would have to see Anthea, or talk to her, at any rate.

'No, really – I've got four, and I don't need them all. Take it!' Against Irina's protests, Lola had packed all the clothes she'd given Irina into an extremely expensive Louis Vuitton Pegase 60 suitcase. She zipped it up and trundled it into the living room. 'There. Now, Leo's going to be here in a few minutes. He's got your ticket and your passport, and he'll take you to the airport. OK?'

Irina nodded. 'Thank you. So many things you give me. It is very kind.'

'Well, look, there's one more thing I want to give you. Before I do, promise me you won't say no, or try to give it back. Please?'

Irina shrugged. 'OK.'

Lola went to her desk, unlocked a drawer and took out an envelope. She gave it to Irina, who opened it. Her eyes widened as she looked at the bundle of $100 bills. 'This money is for books,' said Lola. 'It's for books and whatever else you need to finish your studies. All right?'

Irina took the envelope reluctantly. 'You give me too much.'

'Sweetie, it's small change, compared to what I spend on the useless things in my useless life. Truly. I'm happy to be able to help someone do something worthwhile. Now let's stuff it right into the middle of your suitcase. The zip goes the other way. That's it. Wrap it up in that skirt where no one'll find it.'

The intercom buzzed, and Lola went to let Leo in.

'She's all ready to go,' Lola told Leo.

'Fine. Listen, thank you for looking after her.'

'I've enjoyed having her here. Now that I know what she's been through, I just wish I could have done more. I mean, I think of all the other girls who get tricked and duped and finish up doing what she did. It's horrible.'

'There are organisations who are always on the lookout for volunteers. There's something called the Poppy Project, I believe, that helps people like Irina. You could give it a try.'

'Really? I just might,' said Lola thoughtfully, 'God knows, I've got enough time on my hands.'

'I'll look into it for you, if you like.' Leo gave her a couple of quick kisses. 'Thanks again.' He turned to Irina. 'Come on, let's get going – the traffic can be hell on Saturdays.'

Leo drove Irina to the airport, and took her to the check-in desk. He noticed her glancing around nervously as she stood in the queue, and said, 'Don't worry – Viktor isn't here looking for you. That's over, I promise.' She smiled and gave a little sigh, and he added, 'Do you intend to do anything about Viktor when you get back? Go to the police?'

Irina looked horrified. 'No! He have bad friends. I do not say anything. I cannot.'

Between them, thought Leo, he and Irina were letting a very nasty piece of work off the hook. There was no moral justification, he supposed, except self-interest – the ultimate justification.

Driving back from the airport, Leo thought about Anthea. She'd talked to Lucy, that little drama was over, and now everything, for her, was as it had been. Could it be, for him? He reflected on what Anthony had said of him earlier – that one person would never be enough. No doubt he'd thought it a perspicacious observation. The ironic thing, too, for Leo, Anthony could be that one person. But as things were... Leo drummed his fingers absently on the wheel as the traffic began to slow ominously. As things were...

The traffic came to a complete standstill. Leo tuned into the traffic news. An accident was blocking two lanes of the M4, with two miles of tailbacks already building up. Leo sat thinking for a few minutes, then picked up his mobile phone and tapped in Anthea's number. She answered on the second ring.

'Hi, it's me,' said Leo. 'Sorry if I was a little abrupt last night. I really had had a bad week.'

'Don't worry. We both got a good night's sleep. At least, I hope you did.'

'Kind of. What are you doing tonight?'

'Seeing you, I hope.'

'You hope correctly.' There was a pause. 'I'm glad Lucy spoke to you. I've rather missed you.'

'Well, that's sweet, given that it's only been a few days. Anyway, *I* had to speak to *her*, and drag the truth out of her.'

'We'll talk about it later. I'll pick you up around eight, shall I?'

'Eight is fine. But I made Lucy a promise we wouldn't talk about it. Or rather, about her. And I always keep my promises.'

'Very commendable. In that case, I want you to promise that when I see you later – '

Anthea listened as Leo elaborated. 'That is so depraved! Where do you get these ideas?'

'I don't know,' said Leo, smiling. 'They just come to me.'

On Monday morning, Leo strolled into chambers in a buoyant mood. He and Oliver had had a terrific day on Sunday, savouring the delights of the London Eye and lunch at TGI Friday's, and Rachel had been on her best, civil behaviour when he'd dropped him off. On top of that, Saturday evening with Anthea had been as unwholesome and pleasurable as he'd anticipated. Anthony was right. Serious relationships were definitely a bar to true enjoyment of life.

'Morning, Mr Davies!' called out Felicity in passing. She was wearing a new cashmere sweater with a plunging V-neck, evidently designed to keep Henry on his toes.

''Morning, Felicity. Nice sweater. How was your weekend?'

'Lovely. I'm right off celibacy. I'll pop up and tell you about it later. How was yours?'

Leo hesitated, then said, 'Interesting. Interesting and varied.'

Leo spent most of that morning in meetings convened to deal with the aftermath of Maurice's resignation, and to discuss the future of 5 Caper Court. The departure of Roger and the handful of other junior tenants would leave something of a hole, and despite a promising batch of pupils currently in the pipeline, Leo decided a recruitment drive might be in order. It was just before one, when he was going out to lunch, that he met Michael on the stairs, an early edition of the *Evening Standard* in his hand.

'I was just on my way to see you,' said Michael, handing him the paper. 'Have you seen this?'

Leo read the headline *'Magnate found gassed in car'* then scanned the opening paragraph: *'The construction tycoon Sir Dudley Humble was found dead in his car at a remote spot in Surrey early this morning. He appeared to have died from carbon monoxide poisoning. Sir Dudley was the head of Humble Construction Ltd, a firm which he established in the early 80s and brought to great success in the 1990s, but which had lately suffered setbacks through a number of cancelled contracts and failed bids. In addition to his heavy financial losses, Sir Dudley had recently been questioned by police investigating the ongoing cash-for-peerages scandal.'*

'Christ,' murmured Leo.

'I know – bit of a shock. Did he seem like the suicidal type?'

'Difficult to say,' replied Leo, thinking of Viktor Kroitor's last words to him two days ago. He rather doubted that Sir Dudley had died by his own hand. 'Mind if I hold on to this?' he asked Michael.

'Be my guest. I'll catch you later.'

Leo carried on downstairs, and went into the clerks' room, looking thoughtful.

'Anything up, Mr D?' asked Henry.

'Have a look at this.' He showed the paper to Henry, who gave a low whistle. A sudden thought occurred to Leo. 'Have we been paid yet on the Humble Construction Case?'

Henry tapped at his keyboard and glanced at the computer screen. 'We've issued a fee note.'

Leo nodded. 'Chase it up, would you?'

As he left chambers, musing on Sir Dudley's untimely death, Leo felt a momentary touch of guilt. Maybe if he'd played his hand differently, gone to the police early on, the man might be alive now. Embroiled in an unseemly scandal, but alive.

But in the game which Sir Dudley had chosen to play, there were no rules, no moral outcomes. There was only self-preservation, decided Leo, as he strolled through the Temple, past the buildings and gardens lying serene and timeless in the autumn sunshine.